Enigmatic Mate

Claire Kempler

Contents

1. Is it Mate? — 1

2. Meeting eachother — 5

3. Let me go — 9

4. Tribal wild girl — 14

5. Damn! — 19

6. Positive step — 23

7. Tamaiti — 28

8. Mate bond — 32

9. Jake's advice — 36

10. Trust — 41

11. Excuse me! — 46

12. Next step — 51

13. On the count of Three — 55

14. Scared — 58

15. Her territory — 62

16.	Heartless Humans	67
17.	Three days	72
18.	Not without my mate	76
19.	Aroha yes Vincent	80
20.	Happiness	85
21.	Guilt	90
22.	Traitors	94
23.	Challenge	97
24.	The fight	102
25.	The fight part 2	106
26.	True Queen	110
27.	The Ritual.	115
28.	Training camp	120
29.	Missing her.	125
30.	Epilogue	132

Is it Mate?

----

2 nd Nov 2021

    "Happy Birthday to you... Happy Birthday, dear uncle Vinci. Happy Birthday to you..."

I tried to open my sleepy eyes, hearing her singing in not so soothing voice. She has been creating a disturbance in my sleep from the day she stepped in Southern moon pack. And now she has two little monkeys in her gang who were merrily jumping on my bed.

"Don't you have anything better to do so early in the morning" I got hold of those Chipmunks and cuddled them to sleep with me.

"What can be more important than your birthday, that too your 18th birthday." She argued with her hands on her hips.

"Can't a person sleep on his birthday. " I implied.

"Aren't you excited? It's your 18th birthday. You could meet her today..." She came and sat on the bed.

"IF. If she is in this pack." I tried to take hold of the little guy who was wiggling out of my arms.

"Ya so get up and go out.. Find her?" She insisted.

"What if she is underage still and will take me years to meet her?... what's the fuss, Jia. She will come to me if not today, then tomorrow." I countered.

"You know who she is right? You hacked the council database, isn't it." She looked at me with accusative eyes.

"Oh my sweet Luna, no one knows about the mates until they find each other." She slapped my arm.

"Whatever. Forget mate, you should be excited about your birthday at least"

"I am not a kid like you" I jested.

"What...I am a...Dani and mini... TICKLE..." she yelled and all three of them jumped on me and started tickling me.

"What is happening here? What's the ruckus about?" Great, just he was missing here.

"Daada....Daada." both traitors ran to their father, and so did their mom.

My big Bro. The big bad Alpha of Southern moon pack, Richard Stanford, goes mushy around these three. He scooped his kids up together and hugged his mate. No longer, they were kissing loudly.

"Goddess, what the hell." I mumbled.

"Can you please take your family lovydovyness outside my room." I suggested that earned my brother's focus on me, and he scrunched his nose.

"Warrior Vincent Stanford, you are still in bed!" I rolled my eyes at him. Jia whispered, 'it's his birthday today' in his ears, as if I won't be able to hear.

"So? Who said you have the liberty of sleeping late on your birthday. Anyway Happy Birthday." He brooded.

"Thank you, Alpha, am honored."

"Come Luna, we have things to discuss." He smirked at Jia and went away with giggling pups.

"Come down soon, we are cutting the cake because you are not available in the evening." Jia informed me.

"Yes I am going out with my friends to our cabin in the woods."

"Ya that, so let's celebrate now. Anyway it's noon, you wasted half of your birthday."

Jia Davis Stanford, Luna of Southern moon pack, still so innocent naive and caring.

Hmm, you are now 18 warrior Vincent Stanford. I told myself. Soon I will be going to the Alpha academy for 2 years for training and then...then bro is going to give me 1/3 of his pack to run as an Alpha. Huff. I just hope I can handle all the responsibility, and I Hope I don't get my mate until then. So, now enjoy your day and rest of the remaining time. Mate can wait.

We had just reached the cabin after the celebration back home. Thankfully, my mate was not in the pack. I want a mate, no doubt in that, but it just gets a bit messy. I see my pack members with their mates they love them endless, ready to even die and kill for their mates. They turn into soft love sick puppy and me...I don't need all this as of now.

It was just four of us. Me, my soon-to-be beta Dylan, my gamma, Hunter and my head warrior, Wayne. We are thick of friends, all still without mates.

It was a beautiful night with skyful of stars. Moon goddess draped us in her alleviating light. We were sitting around the campfire relaxing and joking with eachother when a very strong smell hit me. It smelled like sandalwood, Strong and soothing. Does it mean what it means?

"Guys, I smell something very pleasant, and it's pulling me towards it..." I sniffed deeper.

"Oh fuck it's your mate" Hunter choked on his beer.

"No ways" Wayne said, looking around.

"Yo buddy, go for it, she must be near somewhere." Dylan suggested.

"Lets go and check." We stood up and started moving towards the dense trees in the direction of that scent, which was getting stronger to the point of intoxicating. With every step, I took on the damp roots filled earth, I was growing restless.

Something stirred in my head.

'Wakey wakey sleepy head. Something caught your attention?' I asked my wolf.

He stood up in full swing. 'That smell!"

'Aldrich? Is it mate." I asked, moving further in the forest.

'Oh! YES! SURE IT IS.' he beamed.

'Al, something is not right' my restlessness was increasing unexplainablely, now mixed with fear.

____

Meeting eachother

We moved deeper into the woods, following the scent. She kept moving, and then we heard a few more steps running behind her. We even caught few voices of men speaking.

I then realized she was being chased, she was followed by some people. What the hell. That explains the fear and anxiety. My first instincts were to kill those who dared to harass my mate.

"Is she being chased, there are definitely more humans around." Wayne spoke,

"What are humans doing in our territory?" Dylan interjected.

"Your mate is human." Wayne said. It was my least of concern right now that my mate was human. The only thought running through my mind was to keep her safe.

"Wayne and hunter go take care of those humans" I ordered my head warrior and my gamma.

"Dal you come with me." We moved towards my mate.

And...I saw her. Couching near a tree, holding a sharp knife in her hand. I could feel her fear, but at the same time I also felt her determination to slauter who dared to get near her.

'Mate is scared' Al was worried.

'I figured that.' I replied, moving to get closer to her.

'Wait, let me out and meet her' Aldrich suggested.

'Are you mad, out of your senses? She will be scared of a fiery tall wolf. She is human.' he has seriously lost it.

'As of now, she is more scared of humans. An animal mate will make her feel secure,' he quipped.

'Ya right. She will feel secure when a huge wolf with dark grey fur and golden eyes will approach her.' I rolled my eyes at him.

'What do you think? She will see you once and fall in love with your chiseled jaws and black hair on which you apply tons of gel to settle, or she will be mesmerized with your dull forest green eyes that you keep rolling, or your 'know it all' attitude will make her come running towards you.'

'Yes, that's what's gonna happen, just wait and watch. My looks can charm anyone. I will be her knight in shining armor.'

'Try your luck.' he scoffed.

As I took a step out of my hiding place and came into her view, she got up quickly, seizing the knife in air ready to kill. The way she was holding the knife and was in killing stance, no doubt she was a fighter. When my eyes landed on her face, I was awestruck. Her jet black hair was flowing lightly in the air. Her eyes matched her dark hair, they stared at me with confusion. Her dusky skin was adorned with some tattoo on forehead and chin. She was not much tall, but her lean figure made her stand tall. To me, she was like moon goddess herself standing in front of me, mesmerizing me. She, too, must have felt the bond as her brows furrowed, and her head tilted a bit, her hands holding the knife dropped a bit.

'MATE' Aldrich beamed loudly.

"Woah,! she is feisty and human" Dylan jested

"Relax, we are not gonna harm you." I tried to assure her.

But next instance, she pointed her weapon at me.

"Kaua koe e whakatata mai ki a au." She said. She was very attentive and followed my every move with her eyes.

I didn't get anything of what she said, but I had never heard a voice so sweet.

'Interesting'. Al smirked.

"Hey, it's Ok, cool down. You are safe now. Put that knife down." I pleaded with my hands in surrender.

"Māku koe e whakamate." She hissed.

"Put the weapon down, you will injure yourself." I chided. I was worried she will hurt herself.

"Kia mawehe atu i a au, kai te whakatūpato ahau i a koe." She screamed and swiped her knife in front of me.

Goddess! How do I make her understand, and what language is she speaking.

"What is she saying" Dal whispered in my ears.

"How do I know" I was honest. I didn't know what she was communicating.

"YOU DON'T KNOW?" He half yelled.

"Yes, I don't know for once." I huffed."We need to carry her by force, she won't comply."

"Oh man! You want me to touch your mate." Dal snickered.

"Hey Vinci, we scared away those guys. They had guns, seems to be something dangerous." Hunter mind linked me. I had to take her with me to pack house. She is not safe.

"Ok guys, Wayne and you both come from behind and hold her. Dal and I will approach from front. But be gentle, don't harm her" I warned them in our group mind link.

"She is the one who is with a knife here." Dal snorted.

____

"Kaua koe e whakatata mai ki a au." - Don't you dare come near me.

"Māku koe e whakamate." - I will kill you.

"Kia mawehe atu i a au, kai te whakatūpato ahau i a koe." - Get away from me, I am warning you.

Now you know what she said, but our poor Vinci is still clueless.

Vote, Comment, Follow.

Let me go

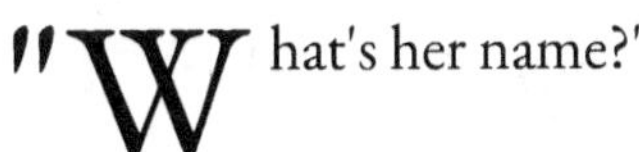

"**W**hat's her name?"

"I don't know"

"How old is she?"

"I don't know...maybe my age."

"Where is she from?"

"I don't know"

"Is she a Rouge?"

"I. Don't. Know."

"Vincent?" She huffed. I know the 'Know all' of our pack was totally clueless about his mate. Difficult to digest.

"Jia." I had woken her up through mindlink after bringing my mysterious mate at the pack house. She is the only one who could understand and can handle the situation. Rest all would have reacted weirdly. My mom and Bro were out of limits.

"Where is she?" She asked curiously.

"That. I know." I gestured her to move towards my room with a smile.

"You have kept her in your room!" She questioned with her brows wide up entering inside my room. Ya because I don't let anyone in my room easily.

"Vinci, she is...."

"Human, I know, and I realize you don't like human mates..." I tried to explain.

"It's not that I don't like them. It's just that... it's not fair to throw them in our dangerous, dominating world." She sympathized. I know that it's difficult, but I can't help it now I have a human mate. Deal with it.

"Why have you tied her up? Goddess.." she glared at four of us. She is the kindest Luna our pack has ever had.

"You don't know, she is a feisty wild cat. We four huge werewolves were finding it difficult to handle her..." A shiver went across my body, remembering how she came upon us all ninja style. We were easy on her thinking she is a human girl, but she had no mercy. We had cuts all over us. I had to strike her neck to make her unconscious.

"She is beautiful... "Jia expressed. That gave me a blush. She is indeed breathtaking with her dusky smooth skin with tattoos and long black hair tied in multiple tiny plates leaving few strands free. She is fit and slim with right curves, her full lips were pinkish and pouted. A pure beauty with intoxicating sandalwood smell, and she is all mine.

She stirred a bit, gaining her senses.

"Oh goddess..." Dylan scooted behind me, fearing her reaction. Hunter, him and Wayne went and stood near the door. She will be one fearsome Luna, for sure. I chuckled at their antics.

She started thrusting on the ropes once she realized that she was bound by them.

"Kātahi te reinga, whakawāteatia ahau ināianei." she shrieked.

(What the hell, free me now.)

"He pūpū pōrangi koe, i mauria mai ahau e koe ki hea. Māku koe katoa e whakamate, ka whakawātea noa iho ahau." Goddess knows what she shouted. Her tone definitely was threatening.

(You bunch of idiots, where have you brought me. I will kill you all, just set me free.)

"Relax no one will harm you." Jia tried to talk to her."What language she is speaking?" She whispered asked, leaning towards me. I shrugged in response.

"How do we communicate with her then?"

"Go figure" I jested, earning a glare from her.

"Tukuna mai i ahau" my mate kept yelling

(Let me go)

'Set her free, she is hurting her self' Al reasoned. Before I can move, Jia was removing the ropes. I know she is very well qualified to defend herself if my mate pounced on her. But my mate got up with lighting speed and stood flushed to the wall, rubbing her sore wrists and glaring at all of us with her black eyes. Her focus went on the glass of water placed on the side table. She gulped visually, wanting to drink it.

"Relax we are friends, not your enemy. We intend no harm. Just relax." Jia offered her glass of water. She drank it as if parched for days.

"Get some food, she must be hungry too."

"I ...I will get it." Dylan rushed out.

"Are you hungry? do you need anything?" Jia asked with care.

"Tukuna mai i ahau" she whispered lowly. Her eyes filled with fear and dread. I felt like embracing her and making her feel safe, but she will be more terrified.

(Let me go.)

"What's your name?" Jia was trying her best to get some answers from her, but we were unable to understand her language.

"Tukuna mai i ahau, Tēnā koa" she kept mumbling.

(Let me go, please.)

Jia said all of our names, pointing fingers at us and then at her to make her understand what we were asking, but she just keeps looking at her. Jia huffed and did the same exercise again.

She started with herself, placing her hand on her heart, "JIA...HUNTER... WAYNE..." Just then Dylan came with food. Jia pointed at him... "DYL AN... VINCENT.... VINCENT." She said my name twice and my mate's eyes fell on me for few seconds and went back to Jia. 'And yours?" She pointed at my mate with raised eyebrows...but she didn't reply...

"Ok, forget it, eat something. You must be hungry" she passed the plate of fruits towards my mate.

"Aroha" came a small voice"ko tōku ingoa Aroha." She said, pointing towards herself.(My name is Aroha)

My heart skipped a beat.Aroha what a beautiful name.

'AROHA.' Al smirked.

Sorry, sorry for the late update. I will try my best update regularly.

And sorry if I am writing the other language wrong. I am totally dependent on google for it.

Please vote, comment and follow if you enjoy reading my stories.

Tribal wild girl

My head was throbbing, why the hell I had to face such a situation? Can't I get a simple mate who is a beautiful werewolf from my pack, and who can read, write and speak English? No moon goddess thought of going creative for me. Let's be different with Vinci, let's give him a human mate. Oh! what's fun in just that now? Let's add some spice. Let her be from some farfetched land where they speak some weird language. See now it fun.I had shifted from my room to my study as my mate was there, and I am sure she won't appreciate my company as yet.

'Relax, it's not that grim of a situation you are in.' Al connoted. 'Have you ever thought about me...She. Doesn't. Have. A. WOLF! Just think about it, whom do I connect with? Where is my mate?' he agonized.

He was right, but I am so not gonna accept it. You can call it Ego, I call it co-existing.

'There is no point in highlighting who is in the more grave situation. We rather work on solution.' I suggested.

'Your mate, your problem. When you figure out how to communicate with her and tell her who you are and after that, if she is still around.... let me know. I will gladly introduce myself. Until then, do not distribute. He yawned and went to sleep. Bloody bastard.

What can be done? Should I ask bro or dad to help me out...NaaahhhAgain, it's not ego, just co-existing...

"Hey buddy, any progress?" Dylan came in my study and asked, picking up an apple from the bowl kept on my table. I looked at him in disbelief.

"What progress? You are asking me? Who is the Alpha here?" I howled and towered over him.

"Y...You" he stuttered, taken back with my sudden outrage.

"And who is the beta? I yelled again.

"M..m..Me?"

"So who will find the solution?" I refuted.

"Me...Me?"

"Good now go and find the solution"

"Okay...chill...." He went out to come back in 2 minutes. I rolled my eyes at his behavior.

"Where exactly do I go to find the solution?" He probed. I should reconsider my decision of making him my beta.

"Go and find Hunter and Wayne" I scoffed at him.

"They have a solution?" He seemed offended.I squinted my eyes at him and added a growl for the effect. He dashed out searching for others. After some time, all of them were standing in front of me.

"Did you find anything about the humans who were following her?" I asked Hunter.

"No, but I am working on it." He replied with a long face. We better find the answer. Who is she, where is she from, why goons were chasing her, and what was she doing in the forest? I huffed. It's a long list.

"From her attire and tattoos, I think she belongs to some tribe." Wayne suggested. I figured that.

"Tribal wild girl, huh?" Dylan teased, making me annoyed.

"Find how many human tribes are there around us, near our territory, and what language they speak. And if possible, please find someone who can speak and understand those languages"I informed them with frustration.

"Hey guys?" Jia entered my study with her two chipmunks. They ran and settled themselves on my lap. I love these two with my life, they are the cutest thing ever to come in this world. No doubt Kevin is cute too, but well...blood is blood.

"Vinci..." She said looking everywhere besides at me. Something is wrong.

"Umm... Richie knows... about.... about... Aroha...I didn't tell him, I sw ear...." she tried to convince me without help. Of course, how can she hide anything from her mate?

"And...ummm"

"Now what?" I growled, making Dani and mini go running towards their mom.

"Luna Joyce also knows." she whispered.

Fcuk...that means the whole pack knows by now.I glared at Jia.

"Don't look at me like that. I was just in your room to give her breakfast. She was happily playing with Dani and Mini when they both came in, and then I had to...tell ....them." she sighed.

"Vincent Stanford in my office now" Bro called through mind link.

"Great now bro is calling me in his office. Anyway, he would have known. I can't hide her forever. Wayne, come with me, you both keep check on her." Jia gave me a tight lipped smile.

I entered Alpha Richard's office. Mom and dad were already there.

"Warrior Vincent, can you explain why have you sneaked in a human in my pack?"

"She is my Mate" I seethed, clenching my fist. I don't know why I was so angry.

"Weren't you supposed to inform the Alpha or ask his permission before bringing her in our territory, as per the protocol?"

"I informed Luna..."

"Of course you informed Luna. I will deal with her later" he mumbled, the last part making me frown.

"She is not at fault. I asked her to keep the information to herself for the time being and..."

"Look, Vinci, it's dangero..."

"She is not in your room" Wayne mind linked me.

WHAT? I stood up with concern. Where did she go?

"What happened?" Bro asked.

"She escaped. She is not in my room" I told him

"Go find her before she witnesses something." He rubbed his brow in apprehension.

I ran out of the office towards my room. As I turned the corner, her scent was the strongest behind me. She was behind me. I knew it, but before I could turn, there was a sharp knife held at my neck.

"Kaua e neke"

Damn!

D aniel and Damien

Vincent's pov

I ran out of the office towards my room. As I turned the corner, her scent was the strongest behind me. She was behind me. I knew it, but before I could turn, there was a sharp knife held at my neck.

"Kaua e neke"

(Don't Move)

"Nāu ahau i mau mai ināianei, māu ahau e tango" she fumed.

(You brought me here now, you will take me out)

"Ok relax, I surrender." I said, holding my hands in the air. Fully aware that she can't understand what I was speaking but could understand the gesture.

She nudged me to move forward.

"Tangohia ahau i konei"

(Take me out of here)

"Sweetheart, I don't know what you are saying. Like, are you taking me hostage to get away from here?" I started walking a bit with a frown. Is my mate threatening to kill me and run away from here...?

"Mauria ahau ki te ngahere, me hoki au ki te kāinga. Me māharahara taku whānau" there was worry in her voice. Why didn't I had hobby of learning new languages instead of gadgets.

(Take me to the forest, I need to go home. My family must be worried)

"Look take it easy, okay. Please, baby, I don't want to hurt you." How do I do this without letting her know about me. I mind linked Bro about our location and to come from behind and take hold of my mate. I mean knife.

'Just look at our mate. I love her, hah? She is dangerous. You are dead human.' Al snickered.

'Shut up' I scoffed at him internally.

I tried to turn and the edge of the knife sliced through my skin and blood started leaking down.

She gasped, looking at what she had done

"Tirohia tāu i mahi ai. I kī atu ahau kia kaua koe e neke. Aue! e te Atua, kai te toto koe. Pōrangi" she yelled with concern and what is pōrangi?? She... she cussed me? I was not worried about the injury, but if she noticed that I could heal real fast she would be suspicious.

(Look what you did. I told you not to move. Oh! god, you are bleeding. Idiot)

'Al, don't heal me...'

'As you wish. ' he cuts my words always

'Till ...she is around.' he is annoying.

Soon, bro came from behind her and snatched the knife from my mate's hand before she could even realize it. She stood there stunned, glaring at bro.

"Human, no one dares to harm my pack members and you...you harmed my brother...if you were not his mate..." Bro warned her in his alpha tone.

"Bro... She can't understand anything." I rolled my eyes.

"That's why I am saying, you, dumbo." He chuckled. Seriously?

"Ko wai a ia ināianei? Kai te tangata tonu a ia?" She said detested.

(Now who is he? Is he even human?)

"I pēhea tō mahi i tēnā? I hohoro tēnā" she said facing bro with folded arms.

(How did you do that? That was fast)

"I am sorry I am taken." Bro told her as if she proposed him and it made me roll my eyes again. Who made him alpha? Just then Jia came with Dani and Mini. If you still have not figured, Dani that is Daniel Richard Stanford and Mini that is Damien Richard Stanford are identical twin pups of Bro and Jia. Don't ask me about the nickname. It's Jia's doing. They are future Alphas of Southern moon pack and moon of our lives. They are tooooo adorable. They have brown hair just like Jia and green eyes just like their dad. Actually green eyes run in our family.

"Love, can you take her inside." Bro told Jia.

Jia placed her hand on Aroha's shoulder, but she jerked it off. That angered me and bro. No one insults our Luna, but Jia being Jia told us to relax through mindlink. Dani took hold of Aroha's hand, and she went with him, stomping her feet.

"Nāu i tūpāpaku taku mahere"She glared at bro and went away mumbling something.

(You ruined my plan).

"She seems to be upset with me. You better find some solution to this, and why aren't you healing?" Alpha walked away saying that.

"Al?"

"Okayyyy. Derek told me already." Derek is Bro's wolf. He is an Alpha wolf with special powers.

I huffed at my situation. My mate, love of my life, was holding a knife at my neck. What more could be disheartening? The one who should love me is not bothered to even hurt me. I need to find a way to communicate with her....how do I do it...damn...Damn...ya Damn. Why didn't I think of it earlier.

____

Here is a new chapter hope you enjoy it. I know it's small but will be back soon.

Please comment, vote and follow

Positive step

"What the hell is all this?" Jia asked with a frown as she entered the library, where I had set up all the gadgets, believing that no one visited the library.

"The solution" I replied, connecting all the wires to the devices

"Solution? It looks like a whole mess of a problem." She said, looking around.

"If you say so. Can you please bring Aroha here?" That made her stare at me. I know no one wants to deal with my mate.

"I will try." She went away saying that.

"Who was she?" My friend Nathan asked. He is here to help me, and all these gadgets belong to him. He was my senior in high school, and now he is in college. We were part of the same club and become good friends. He was called the gadget man. Nathan was your typical geek guy with spectacles and loads of intelligence. I know bringing a human into our territory is risky, but I had to put up with the idea.

"My...my sister-in-law," I told him

"She called my gadgets a problem." It disheartened him a bit.

"Ummm..."

"What is this shit?" Bro came in and scoffed, looking around.

"Hey, man. This ain't no shit, ok." Nat hollered.

"One more human in my territory without my consent." Alpha Richard glared at me. Soon all my friends came too.

"What is all this crap?" Dylan snored!

"Hey hey hey, what is the problem with you people? Are you illiterates? This place is full of weirdos." Nathan outraged.

"Nat..." I tried to calm him. He better not shout at the Alpha.

"They are calling my invention shit and crap and..and a problem." He grunted.

"Chill buddy. Who are you?" Dalton asked, sniffing him.

"I am Vinci's mate" Nat nested, and I facepalmed myself.

"WHAT?" There was a chorus around that made Nat flinch. He had this unbelievable expression on his face.

"SCHOOL MATE!" I clarified.

"Oh! I thought..."

"You don't give your brain much trouble," I told Dal, shaking my head

"Do you care to explain what is all this and what are you planning on?" I huffed at bro's sarcasm.

"Okay, let me explain. This is The human analyzer invented by my friend here, Nathan. He is head of our Technology club. He invented this device that helps to get the details of human origins and their characteristics based on their DNA structure. In simple language, we will scan Aroha and the computer over here will give all her details. Like her age, her origin, her health statistics..."

"Seriously, can this thing do that?" Alpha asked curiously.

"Yes, and we also have a translator device, again invented by our dear friend Nathan." I tried to boost Nat's confidence.

"Impressive. So what are we waiting for?" I know Bro had his full interest now.

"We are waiting for Aroha" I mumbled. I hope she cooperates.

"Waiho mai ki a au ngā taniwha" My mate is here.

(Leave me you monsters)

"Purua ahau ki tēnei wā don't"

(Put me down right now) an uproar reached us before I saw two warriors bringing my mate dangling and withering between them. The sight made me growl. Jia soon followed behind. I questioned her with my eyes, to which she shrugged.

This is going to be very difficult.

I told Nat to record her sound, so we could fetch the language through the internet and then help us translate.

I motioned those warriors to place Aroha on a chair in front of the scanner. They were having a difficult time doing so. My mate was not ready to comply.

"Did you get the language?" I inquired Nat, who was monitoring the results.

"Not yet"

"Tīkina ahau ki konei. Māku koe katoa e whakamate"

(Get me out of here. I will kill you all)

"Got it" Nat boomed, clapping his hands.

"Great, put on the translator."

"Done."

"Aroha calm down, we won't hurt you" I spoke in English but soon a computerized voice spoke behind me. Stunning everyone, even Aroha who was shocked.

"Aroha, marino, e kore mātou e mamae i a koe"

"Me pēhea tēnei e kōrero ai i taku reo" she pointed towards the speaker as if scared of it.

(How can this speak my language?)

Again a computerized voice told us what she spoke. Aroha gasped, But I was so happy. Now I can communicate with my mate and know her better. I had so many questions for her and I was getting impatient to get all the answers. At least we had taken a positive step in our relationship.

"Ka taea e koe te tuku atu i a au ki konei ināianei. E hiahia ana ahau ki te haere ki taku iwi, ki taku whānau. Ko te tikanga kia tatari rātau ki a au. He aha koe i kawe mai ai i a au ki konei"

She said in a stressed voice, understanding what we were trying to do. She too wanted us to understand her.

"Can you let me go from here now. I want to go to my people, my family. They must be waiting for me. Why did you bring me here?"

Her people? Her family. She wants to go...but how can I let her leave? She is my family, my life, my mate. The one that is made for me, just for me.

"Hey Vinci, I have all the details" Nat interjected my thoughts. As Aroha was busy in getting out of shock, Nat had scanned her face to get her details.

Hey everyone, I hope you like this chapter. All the device and gadgets mentioned are just my imagination. I don't know if such things exist or not.

Do let me know your thoughts on the same.

Vote comment and please follow me if you enjoy reading my stories.

Tamaiti

"Hey Vinci, I have all the details" Nat interjected my thoughts. As Aroha was busy in getting out of shock, Nat had scanned her face to get her details.

I dashed towards the screen displaying the data.

Name - Aroha (we had to feed it in computer)Skin tone - DuskyEye color - blackish brownHair color - blackFacial authenticity - Nu Tiranian (what does that mean?)Age - 20 (what?)

"Twenty? She is older than you." Dylan snickered behind me. I turned around to notice three more heads leaning into the computer screen.

"Interesting." Alpha sassed.

'Hey, can you let me go now. I need to go home." Aroha had recovered from here shock and spoke impatiently. Though she was speaking in her language, we could hear it in English. Advantages of technology.

She wants to go home, How do I let her go? Isn't this supposed to be her home. A home with me, but she wants to go away.

We all were quiet, not knowing what to reply. Everyone had focused their eyes on me. Their eyes hold pity because my mate wants to leave, it gives out her rejection towards me, our bond. But how can I blame her? She knows nothing.

"Look, I need to go. It's urgent. Thank you very much for your hospitality and these...these clothes" she gestured towards the Jia's clothes. I remember she was so unwilling to wear shorts and tshirt...

"but they must be waiting for me..." She continued to convince us, taking the situation as her opportunity to make us understand her situation.

"Where is your home?" Alpha asked, taking the matter in his hands.

"You drop me till forest. I will go from there." I furrowed my eyes at her. She doesn't want us to know where she lives?

"We rescued you from there, why you want to go back. Those goons were behind you." Alpha asked.

"I was on a mission before these kids brought me here. I need to go before we lose them"

KIDS. Who is a kid here? She is just two years elder to me. She can't kid me.

"What mission?" Alpha asked, suppressing the laugh. He was enjoying at my situation.

"Oh! Goddess. Since long, young girls from our tribe were kidnapped. We never found them again. Our whole tribe was distraughted. We were losing young girls, we never knew what happened to them. We made a plan and as per the plan, I got myself kidnapped by them to know their location and purpose."

"Why you? Aren't there capable men in your tribe." I questioned. Why are they sending my mate in this dangerous mission.

"They want girls not men. And I am more than capable than any men." She rolled her eyes as if I had asked her most stupid question.

"Please ignore him and continue."

"Ya so they took me there and what I saw was beyond shocking. They had the huge number of girls, more than my tribe girls whom they force into prostitution and body selling ..."

"Disgusting"

"They treat these girls very badly. These people are not humans, they are animals who tear the dignity of girls."

"Initially, as per the plan, I had to take my girls and leave, but I can't leave the rest of girls there. So I need to get my entire tribe at their place to rescue all of them. I need to go before they send these girls to other continents."

"What the fucking hell. Human trafficking? Prostitiution? This is so dreadful." Alpha hissed. It was indeed horrible thing to do to young girls, and I feel proud of my mate that she was brave enough to help.

She needs to go, only she can rescue them, I know that but what about me. Once she goes away she will never come back...what do I do? I can't live without her...

"Then help her, dumbo. Help her in her mission. Her mission is our Mission. She is mate." Al connoted.

Yes... We will help her...that is the only right way to be with her, to know her and her people.

"We will help you in your mission" I stated.

"You will help me? Can you even fight?" She scrunched her nose, eyeing me up and down.

"Ouch" Jia whispered. She knows my mate is insulting me, but I can't do anything about it.What she thinks? Am I a small kid? I can't fight? She doesn't know who I am.

"Don't worry my people will help you we have the huge number of strong Warriors capable of taking down a huge army." Alpha said proudly.

"You will help me?" She was surprised and relieved, bouncing up and down in excitement.

"Yes we will"

"We need to act fast, get there as soon as possible. I can lead the way" she almost smiled making my heart skip a beat, that was the first time I saw her smile it was beautiful...

"We leave at dawn tomorrow. I will prepare my people. You, too, rest for the time being." Alpha told her leaving with Luna, and she nodded in response.

I wondered how we will communicate during this mission when she called at me.

"tamaiti"

Mate bond

<hr>

V incent Stanford

"We leave at dawn tomorrow. I will prepare my people. You, too, rest for the time being." Alpha told her leaving with Luna, and she nodded in response.

I wondered how we will communicate during this mission, so I went up to Nathan who was busy winding up the whole setup.

"Hey, do you have some small and portable version of translation device. Like something, we can use tomorrow?" I asked Nathan with my fingers crossed. We can't carry this setup with us for the mission, and communication with Aroha is the key of this mission.

"You are so lucky, buddy. I have just something you will need." He gave me ear pods and beamed with arrogance.

"What do I do with this? These are simple ear pods." I asked, taking the box of ear pods and checking them.

"I am shocked that you are asking me this. These are not normal ear pods. You can install any software in them as they are advanced ones. So, you

install the translation software as we already know the language and tada...
You can hear everything your girl says." He rolled his eyes at my silliness

"She...um... She is not my girl....yet" I am sure I was blushing, but he said
my girl?

"Come on, you love her, It's written on your face, and you are helping her
in her mission. That's great." he smirked.

"Umm..." I was speechless. I ran my hand on my face.

"Cool buddy, she likes you too." He said confidently.

"H.. How do you know?" I was baffled. When this nerd geek turned into
love guru?

"The way she looks at you... come on, anybody can see it." He explained. I
blinked twice to confirm that this was Nathan who was saying all this. The
guy who has never approached any girl in college.

"Ok thanks buddy, thanks a lot. I will drop you home." I said, not wanting
to discuss further on the topic with him. We were busy packing things up.

"tamaiti" I heard my mate's voice. Now what is taa..maiti? I turned to face
her. She was standing with folded arms.

(Hey kid) - tamaiti

"E tika ana kia taea e koe te whawhai?" She said.

(Are you sure you can fight?)

"Ki taku whakaaro he pai ake mēnā ka noho anō koe ki te tākaro me ō
taonga tākaro" she made some gestures with her hands and her face gave
some weird expression.

(I think it would be better if you stay back and play with your toys)

Whatever she was saying, it was evident from her smirking lips and arrogant tone that she was making fun of me and was saying something nasty about me. I stepped closer to her and leaned my face near her ear.

"I love you too sweetheart" saying that, I gave her one of my best smile. She furrowed her brows, tempting me to annoy her further.

"I like everything about you. Your hair are like dark night, I want to sleep in them" I took hold of some strands of her black hair and turned them around my finger. She took a step back. I wanted to mention about her plump lips that I wish to kiss so badly but skipped as we had audience.

"Your cheeks are like sun-kissed tomatoes that I want to bite" I stepped closer to her and made a bitting gesture with my teeth. She gave me a death glare.

"Your eyes are like black hole, I want to get sucked in them." I caressed her cheeks as my fingers tingled with her touch and peered in those black orbs. She leaned in my touch a bit, and I was so overwhelmed. Can she feel the bond? But before I can think more into it, she swatted my hand away with a jerk.

"No..noho atu, māku rānei koe e whakamate" She stuttered glaring at me, but I responded with a wink and smirk and that made her furious. She stormed out with the two warriors who had brought her here, tailing behind her.

(S..Stay aa..away or I wil kill you.)

"Oh, my sweetheart, you will kill me one day." I mumbled to myself. I went back to Nathan, he gave me a mischievous smile.

"Take it easy buddy, you scared the poor girl." I smiled at him. If only he knew. My girl is not scared of anyone. Did she really felt the bond and sparks at my touch, because I saw her leaning into my hand but backed off instantly. Do humans feel the bond? Can they feel the tingles and sparks? My head was buzzing with all the questions. Only one person can answer my questions. Brittney. She is human and can clarify my doubts.

I called Hunter through mind link and asked him to drop Nathan. I had to talk to Brittney right now.

"Hey Nathan, I just remembered one urgent work. Hunter will drop you. And thanks, buddy, thanks a lot." I said giving him a side hug.

"It's okay man. Do you seriously have people that can fight, as your brother mentioned? That's strange! Is your brother..."

"Hey, see Hunter is here." I cut him mid-sentence. It's not wise to keep him in our territory for longer and risk our existence.

Hunter came and they left. I made my way towards Brittney's room. It's a bit late in the evening, but I am sure Brittney won't mind.

———————

Hey everyone,

Updates on this story starts from today. Hope you like it.

Please vote and comment. Also follow me for notifications of the updates. You can follow me on instagram with same name

I will try to update regularly as I had kept this story on hold for long.

Thanks

Jake's advice

I made my way to Brittney's room, hoping that Jake won't be there. I don't have anything against him, he is a nice fellow, but he is so stiff with us that it's intimidating at times. Jia told me he was a jovial and funny person. What happened with his pack, may be turned him into this serious, no smile guy. Still, after all these years it feels he has not accepted this pack wholeheartedly.

I knocked on the door and to my dismay, Jake opened the door.

"Warrior, Stanford...how can I help you." See what I always told formal and upright. He must be reading a book, as he had one held in his hand.

"Umm...can I have a word with Brit...um Brittney?" He furrowed his brows at me.

"Whose it baby?" Brit asked from inside.

"Warrior Stanford, he wants to have a...word with you." He replied her, still staring at me with those questioning eyes.

"Who?" Brit came to the door and saw me. "Oh Vinci, it's you. I wondered who warrior Stanford is...come on in." She waved her hand for me to get in.

"Umm...can I..." I requested Jake as he was still standing at the door. He then moved to let me in.

"Thanks" I went near Brittney who was sitting with Kevin on the carpeted floor of their living room. Each room of the pack house is a small apartment with small kitchen, 2 bedrooms and washroom.

"Hey little buddy, how are you? I picked up Kevin, who was coloring some books.

"Vinci, let's do coloring." Kevin quipped.

I placed him down and sat on the carpet of their living room to do the coloring. He was so good at doing this. He had filled out colors so neatly, and I thought I would mess his beautiful art if at all I contributed, but to make him happy I picked the big yellow crayon and started filling the sun picture. Kevin scrunched his nose in dislike and looked at me. I placed the crayon back in the box and smiled at him.

He didn't insist after that. Uff! What will he think of me.

"What you want to talk about" Brittney raised her brows.

"I..um...I wanted to ask you.. something..."

"They do" she replied.

"W..what?" I was so confused.

"Us humans feel the mate bond." She remarked.

"H..How..." How did she know what I wanted to ask.

"How do I know what you want to ask? Off course why else you would want to meet me so late" she shrugged.

"I apologize for disturbing you..." I attested.

"Come on Vinci. We are not going to be so formal now. We feel the bond, Not as strong and clear like you do, but there is definitely a pull and attraction."

"Aroha doesn't feel it, I think?" I sighed.

"Why you think so?"

"Because she talks way rudely with me and always looks at me like I am some dirt." I implored.

"Does she do that with everyone?"

"No..."

"Just with you right"

"Yeah" I nodded.

"Maybe she is in denial" she concluded. As I didn't show any expression, she continued.

"What, I think, is that she feels the attraction and the bond and is confused that why she is feeling these things for a total stranger.There is a conflict between her brain and her heart. Her heart feels the attraction, but her brain doesn't accept it so it's telling the heart to dislike you and so in this conflict she acts rudely to you so that she can tell herself that she is not affected by your presence" she illustrated.

"WHAT." Jake and I yelled together. I didn't get anything she spoke, and I didn't know Jake was listening to us so intently. Brittney rolled her eyes and mumbled 'men' under her breath.

We both were still looking at her, waiting impatiently for the explanation, but she just kept staring at us.

"Forget it, just understand that she feels the mate bond and is definitely attracted to you." She rolled her eyes and me.

"Umm ok...but you said she is in denial...why? I mean, why would she ..." I argued.

"You don't know her, Vinci." She stated as a matter of fact. That hurts."She has a life before you met her, and you know nothing about it. Reason could be anything..." she reasoned.

"Hmm" I was still confused when Jake cleared his throat.

"Listen kid, forget everything. Just go and tell her about us and about her being your mate. Mark her and get done with this. I did the same. Don't keep beating around the bush. It will just prolong the process" He advised. I stood up and sat on the couch next to him.

"Without her consent?" I asked, "Like I just go to her, tell her that I am a werewolf, and she is my mate and just mark her! I don't want to die so young, please" I shuddered.

"No. Never without her consent, but use your charm on her." He smirked.

I looked at him baffled. Did he just say that. He went back to reading his book. I gaped at Brit. She closed my mouth.

"That's real Jake for you" she chuckled.

____

Hey everyone,

Hope you are having good time.

Enjoy the chapter and please vote, comment and follow me

Also follow me on instagram (Curiouswords27)

Thanks

Trust

- -

The whole night, I was thinking about what Brittney and Jake said. Sleep was far from me when I should be resting my body to prepare for the upcoming mission. I was confused about what to think? Why girls behave against their thoughts. If you like someone you just express it, what is this denial and all. That's the reason I never went near girls. They are complicated. More complicated than assembling an IKEA furniture. I never even dated someone. What's the point if you know she is not the one for you.

Next morning we had to report at grounds for the briefing at 4am, and we were going to leave at 5am sharp. As I reached, I saw Alpha and Luna arguing about something. Well, it's nothing new, they are always arguing. I rolled my eyes and went near them.

"I am coming, you like it or not." Jia huffed. Oh! the same old drama. Bro doesn't want her to come with us, and she wants to come, again, nothing new.

"Just think about kids, who will take care of them?" Richard tried to convince Jia

"Seriously! You are saying that in your defense? Well, for your information. There is Brittney and Luna Joyce...Jess"Why you always do this Richie, I am a warrior I need to be there." Jia whined.

"I know you are a warrior, that to a very good one, but you are a Luna too. You have to take care of our pack, our people in my absence. Please understand sweetheart." Bro said while holding Jia's face gentle in his hands.

"W..what if s..something happens to you." She stuttered, holding his hands.

"Nothing will happen to me, baby. We are fighting humans, and we have weapons too AND your brother and best friend are with me. So don't worry"he said joining their foreheads. They were so in love. The way bro talked to Jia Showed how much he loves her.

I moved a bit away and stood next to Jake, who was watching them from far.

"Sweet isn't it?" Jake commented and I nodded in response.

Ya, earlier when bro and Jia indulged in their cozy moment, my reaction was 'what the heck!' but now I find it sweet and can't help imagining me and Aroha in such moments

After the briefing, Bro asked me to get Aroha as we had to leave. I knocked on the door of her room. Which technically is my room...but it's our room now... whatever.

When she opened the door, my heart skipped a beat. She was looking absolutely beautiful like a divine angel, her hair bit wet, and she was wearing her old dress which she had worn when we met. I kept staring at her until her very much annoyed and irritated voice reached my ears.

"HE AHA!" She spoke and soon after the device translated it in English. (WHAT?)

I opened my palms in front of her to take the ear pods which I had readied for the mission. One set for her and one for me. She frowned her brows in confusion at the device. I moved my head and tapped on the pod I was wearing to show her my ears to make her understand its use. But she made no move to take them. I think I will have to do the honor gleefully.

I stepped closer to her, and she glared at me in warning, tilting her head. I picked one ear pod and showed it to her, I took one more step closer to her, and now we were breathing the same air. I could hear her fast beating heart, and it made my heart race too. I tucked some strands of her hair behind the ear with a trembling hand, dreading she would swat them away. But she didn't. I inserted the pod in her ear and did the same with the other one. All the while we were staring at each other. I was totally mesmerized and absorbed by those black orbs. Our bond was getting stronger, I could feel it, I could feel her emotions at times, like right now she was definitely intimidated by our closeness. We were both engulfed in warmth of each other.

She cleared her throat after a few seconds, bringing me out of trance.

"Umm...we can communicate with help of this." I rubbed my sweaty hand on my jeans pearing at her to know if she understood.She nodded and broke our staring contest.

"We need to go" I told her, walking ahead

"Kai hea taku naihi?" She inquired(Where is my knife?)

"Knife?"

"I mauria mai ahau e koe ki konei."(Ya one you took when you brought me here.)

"Oh..oh that. You need it?" We were actually communicating. Thanks to Nathan.

"Me patu ahau, kai te haere tātau mo te riri."(I need to be armed, we are going for the battle.)

"You need not worry. I won't let anything happen to you." I assured her.

"Kaore e taea e au te whakawhirinaki ki a koe ki tōku oranga. E hiahia ana ahau ki taku patu."(I can't trust you with my life. I want my weapon.) Ouch! that hurts. She doesn't trust me.

Al snickered in the back of my head.

'Oh welcome back' I told him rolling my eyes he was absent for so long.

I turned and faced her and took her soft face in my hand. It was quite bold of me, but what boosted my confidence was she didn't push me. I removed the ear pods from her ears because she can't hear what I am going to say. I leaned my forehead to hers, just as bro and Jia had done and sparks erupted in every cell of my body. She stiffed but didn't move.

"I won't let any harm come near you." I whispered "You are so precious to me that I will protect you with my life. You are mine. You don't know that yet, but you are MINE. My mate, the best gift moon goddess gave me. You don't trust me now, but I will do my best to gain it and then a time will come when we will build a future together, a very beautiful future with you me and our kids." I pulled away a bit staring in her eyes, assuring her with my gesture that she is safe with me. I kissed her forehead. My lips tingled with our touch, and then let go of her face. She had closed her eyes, feeling the moment. She definitely felt our bond, and I was so beaming.

I placed the ear pods again in her ears

"Let's go everyone is waiting" I mumbled

"H.. haere atu i a au, i I. M..a.. Ma koe e whakamate."(G..get away from me or I..I w..will kill you.) She pushed me and walked ahead of me.

I chuckled in response, but what she said next broke my heart.

————

Please Vote, comment and follow

Excuse me!

We were 10 of us, including Aroha. She was sitting on the passenger seat, giving directions, while Jake was driving. Me, Alpha and Owen (Beta of Southern Moon Pack) were sitting at the backside. One more SUV was behind us which had Dylan, Wayne, Rick, our best tracker. Susan, she is daughter of our former head warrior and last Hunter. We were going towards the spot from where we had 'kidnapped' – her words not mine' Aroha. From there she will take us to the abandoned building where all the girls are being kept. She had already briefed us about the area and number of men we would encounter. As per her, it was a one-story structure with front and back entrance, each guarded by an armed person. Roof had two guys again armed and four to five men inside monitoring the girls. So, in total not more than 9 to 10 humans who can be taken by a single werewolf but...but we will be fighting them as humans no one by any chance can transform in front of them. Those were the strict instructions from the Alpha.

During the whole ride, I was lost in my thoughts about what Aloha said before leaving.

"Let's get this done so that I can go back to my people and never have to see your face again"

It hit me like a brick. Sh... She will go away after this...once her mission is over, she will be back with her people and then?..what about us? WHAT ABOUT US! How do I convince her that she is my life and I can't survive without her. That her being away from me would kill me slowly. How do I convince my human mate that I am already in love with her after just one week of knowing each other...hah! In fact I love her in spite not knowing anything about her at all... I just don't know what to do about it.

Al whined in my head.

'We should just mark her and never let her go, what's to think so much in this." He said.

'Al please, let me handle it my way' I rolled my eyes at his pathetic suggestion

'Your way! And what is your way? Please enlighten me.' He scoffed.

'I will figure out something.' He snorted and kept quiet. I don't want to force mark her. Never.

"I just hope we are not late!" An electronic voice reached me. She was getting anxious with each passing moment, and I was more worried about aftermath. We will definitely rescue those girls, so it was not of my concern. We had the best team and even though any number of humans is no match to 9 trained warriors, werewolves.

"KA MUTU TE WHAKATŪ. Me tū tātau ki konei." Aroha yelled

("STOP STOP. We need to stop here.")

Jake pressed the break immediately, making all of us jerk forward. Aroha had made the car stop on a small, dirty path. Where were we? I didn't even notice where we were heading.

"The structure is just around this corner" she said pointing towards the curve on the path and I translated for others

'Whose territory is this?' I asked Bro through mind link.

'We are in the human part of the forest.' He told me. All of us got down silently. Rest of Others got down too from their car.

"We will walk towards the spot in groups so that we don't attract their attention. I want everyone to be careful about, you know what. Got it?" Alpha instructed, and We all nodded in response.

"Ok then, Rick, Jake, and Susan you all go first and don't reveal yourself."

"Yes Alpha" they said in unison and went away holding out their guns

Bro glared at their backs, clenching his jaws.

'No one fucking calls me Alpha, get that clear in your heads.' He busted through our group mind link.

"Owen, Dylan, and Wayne, you go next."

They nodded and went away.

"Ok that leaves Me, Vinci, Aroha, and Hunter. We go next." He said getting his gun out.

"She is not coming. It's not safe." I stated pointing towards Aloha who was ready with knife in her hand.

"Excuse me" she snapped after a few seconds

"You will stay in the car until we get back" I warned her.

"Who are you to decide that, and I will be safe in this vehicle?" She grunted with flaring her nostrils.

"It's a bulletproof car, you will be safe in it. I am not discussing it anymore. You will stay here." I whisper yelled at her. Can't she understand. She wants to fight those criminals with just a knife!

"Are you insane by any chance. Who are you to give me commands." She closed her eyes for a second, gritting her teeth and yelled at me.

"I am your Mat..." I snarled but was cut by Alpha.

"Alright there. Stop it both of you. Let her come Vinci." Bro Declared.

"But..." I wanted to argue but then gave up as Al told me to keep mate with us."Fine...but stay close to me" I told her.

She stomped and started moving ahead of us. As we rounded the corner, we saw a ruined one-story structure. It was easy to hide as we were surrounded by tall dry grass, stooping a bit we moved forward.

"Richard" Rick whispered through mind link. We halted on the spot. I took hold of Aroha's arm to make her stop. She frowned her brows at me.

"There are around 25 humans in here, and they are moving everything out. I think they are evacuating. There are huge trailer at the back entrance." He explained.

"25. Aroha said there won't be more than 10." I asked. This is not good.

"One more thing. We are inside the building and there are no girls in here. It's empty."

———————————

Hey everyone.

Sorry for the late update.

Requesting my readers to please give some feedback on the story so far. It will motivate me to update faster.

I genuinely need to know if the story is exciting or not. Please do comment.

Next step

E MPTY! Oh! hell!

Oh! goddess, we are late. That was the very first thought that came in my mind. They must have moved the girls or even would have sold them. How are we going to find them now? And what do I tell Aroha. She will freak out, hate me even more. It will be my fault that I took her away and delayed her mission. Why, there was a hurdle at every step towards my mate. I don't know why we were facing so many obstacles. It is so easy for normal mates, they find each other, mate right after and live happily ever after. That's what I had always imagined.

Now that the girls are missing... We are doomed. No...I am doomed. I huffed.

"Why are we not going inside?" My mate asked. Again this electronic voice, it is so irritating compared to my mate's sweet voice. I hope this won't be our source of communication through life. I glanced at her, and she was looking at us suspiciously.

"We are waiting for the signal from others." Bro replied, but she was not convinced and kept staring at us with doubt.

"What are our orders, Alpha?" Jake asked through mind link.

"How many girls are there?" bro asked Aroha.

"tekau ma rima" she said with her frown intact.

"15" I translated. 15 girls who could be anywhere in the world if they had sold them already. How will we track them.

"Rick, can you track the girls with their smell?"

"There are too many smells, and I don't know which one to focus on?" He admitted.

"Just see if you can find something that could possibly belong to girls so we can get some clue." Bro suggested.

"There are some clothes in the corner, I will get them." Susan said. That could definitely lead us somewhere if...if those clothes belong to one of the girls. But again, why any girl's clothing was discarded in the corner was a freaking thought in itself.

"Ok Rick, you focus on tracking, and we will handle the humans." Bro ordered.

"Vinci, what is your mate doing?" Owen pointed out. Their group was stationed near the warehouse. I turned towards her direction to get the shock of my life. She was not beside us. Didn't I clearly asked her to be with us. While We were engrossed in thinking and planning the next step, Aroha decided to take matters in her hands as she was done relying on us.

"What the fuck. Where is she?" I panicked. The thought of something happening to her was killing. Al was in full attention now, sniffing to get us near mate.

"She is going towards the warehouse" Dylan informed me. I rushed behind her using my werewolf speed. I saw her moving very slowly. I grabbed her waist with one hand and her covered her mouth with the other, so she would not scream. My action was so fast that we lost our balance. Next I know she was right under me, breathing heavily. My anger vanished, looking at her trembling lips. Her heart was beating like crazy, and so was mine. Before I could go stupid and lean in to claim those lips, Bro's voice reached us.

"Are you two ok?" He inquired.

I moved from her and nodded at bro. He glared at Aroha Who sat up, flustered.

"What were you up to? Please stick to the plan. You could have ruined everything." He gritted at her. Al growled in displeasure, but we would never go against our Alpha.

"Mō taku hē""Sorry" she mumbled

"Alpha, I think I found the girls. I can smell them inside the trailer that is parked at the backside." Rick informed through our link.

"Oh great. At least they are still here..." Bro exclaimed. I was so relieved to hear it. Thanks goddess, they were safe.

"What do we do now" I asked.

"Is anyone in the trailer, or is it being guarded?" Owen inquired.

"No, these people are busy in their work." Rick replied.

"Ok. Jake, you go to Rick. Both of you take the trailer away from here while we distract humans. Wait for my signal. Everyone moves towards Susan." Alpha gave out orders.

I took hold of Aroha's arm, and we moved slowly inside the structure, where Susan was hiding behind a broken wall. From here we could see all the activities going on in the backside. Humans were loading crates and crates of something in to the trucks. Jake had already moved out.

"How do we distract them" Susan asked.

"We attack"

————————

Hey everyone.

Thank you so much for being patient with me. I know the updates are very slow and short but I am trying my best. I hope you enjoy this chapter.

Please voe and comment

On the count of Three

'Attack? Like we just open fire?' I inquired through our mindlink, not liking the idea at all.

'That is the only way to get their attention and leave the coast clear for Jake and Rick to get away with that trailer. We don't want them following any of us.' Bro explained.

'But what if they counter strike. They are more in numbers.' I asked getting agitated.

'I know and they will, but what are our options. We need to distract them, that too in a surprise attack. By the time they understand and react we should be able take down half of them.' he elobrated. It seemed to be a great plan unless it may backfire. We can get injured.

'we can handle their bullets, but Aroha what about her? If she gets hit then?' I am getting furious by each passing second. Being werewolves we can survive the bullets but Aroha is human and being my mate, Her protection is my utmost priority. My protective instinct were getting hyper with Al pacing and growling around like ready to attach anyone who even looked at our mate.

"Where are the girls?" Aroha whisper asked in between looking frantically everywhere.All of us were having serious discussion through mindlink about further steps and her question made all of us look at her.

"Umm they...they are in the trailer outside." I replied with a bit stutter.

"How do you know?" She blurted with her brows knitting together.

"Rick found them" I replied not daring to look in her full of doubt eyes . I know I was giving her short answer which frustrated her. But now was not the time to explain her anything.

'As soon as Jake and Rick are out of here you take Aroha and get back to cars we will cover you. Go to our territory. We will handle here. Bro continued to explain his plan after small distraction caused by Aroha.

'I won't leave you all here. These are dangerous people. What if they call more of them.' I can't just go away leaving my Alpha in danger. Fighting rogues or other werewolves seemed so easy now. Atleast we could be in our element and fight back with vigor. But here we have to be extra careful and fight in human forms

'Do you think I can't handle them? I can take them down single handed and you are right this seems to be a whole human trafficking racket. Many influencial people will be involved. I don't want to risk them knowing our identities.'

"What are we waiting for?" Aroha asked again gritting her teeths. I know she is confused like hell. But I will explain her later.

"When I signal you, we start running towards the exit and back to cars."

"But.." she opened her mouth to say something but I stopped her with my finger on my lips.

"Shhh...do as I say" I spoke sternly and she gave me her death glare. We were still crouching against the wall hiding behind it. We need to act fast before they know about us.

"Ok, on the count of three" Alpha's firm voice rang through our mindlink. Everyone of us got alert, our reflexes on stand. I could hear heart beats of each of us, thumping against ribcage.

"One." We took our guns out stretching our hands out. Back exit was some 15 meters from us where all humans were busy in their work. Al was ready in stance to pounce.

"Two." We arranged our positions as per our strategy of fighting. Alpha, beta and head warrior on the front. So Bro, Owen and Hunter were first in line. Behind them were Dylan, Wayne and Susan. And last me, shelding my mate behind me. We were just 2 meter away from front exit. As soon as I get the signal from Bro, I and Aroha will dash out. Hope we...

"And three..."

Scared

- -

A roha

She was definitely thinking in her language but I translated it.

I was scared, so scared. Never in my life, I have been scared of anything. I am not someone who will get scared and sit in a corner. No, not me.

I was not scared as this mad man who was driving this vehicle sitting right beside me like a manic.

I was not scared when I volunteered to go for that mission. When a girl from our tribe went missing first we thought she left with someone. Then the next one went missing, but when Pania went missing with the other two girls we could not sit idle. Pania is my best friend. She is a very soft and naive person, not someone to fight back, and I had to go and get her. Tane was furious with my idea of getting myself kidnapped and then bringing all the girls back. Even my father didn't approve at first. But when Ari went missing, it was the last blow. Ari was just 16. How could they take her? All these incidents shook our whole tribe. All of us were terrified. Families of taken girls were shattered and devastated. I had to stop, whoever was thinking it is easy to take girls from our tribe. We can't live in fear of losing our daughters. As a daughter of the head of the tribe, it is my responsibility to protect my people. When our head adviser Maugham, Tane's father suggested this was the only way then Tane and father supported me.

I was not scared when I went to outskirts of our area at night and was taken immediately. As if they were waiting for me. They took me to an abandoned structure where the rest of the girls were held captive. There I saw more girls from our neighboring tribes too. Pania was crying mess. One of the girls from our neighboring tribe knew their language, so she informed me that these people sell all the captured girls for body selling. I was horrified. Their crime was inhuman and unforgivable. Such people should rot in hell. I assured the girls I will be back to get them away and sneaked out.

I was not scared when out of nowhere three boys kidnapped me and brought me to their land. They spoke the same language as those goons. I was so frustrated that they didn't let me go and delayed me in getting my work done. Finally when we were able to communicate they decided to help me after hearing my problem. These people are different, something is mysterious about them. I can't figure what. Their house is huge where they all live together, they are so strong and fast. Something is definitely unusual about them.

I was not scared when Vincent...he has such a wonderful name... And his team started firing bullets towards goons. We were crouching against the wall, they were staring at each other as if communicating through eyes and discussing something. When I asked, they gave me short and wage answers. all of a sudden they became alert. I don't know how they came to know that girls were in side that huge vehicle. When firing started I clasped my hands on my ears, it was deafening. There were lots of cries and yelling going on. As soon as those goons recovered from the attack, they started firing back and at that moment Vincent took hold of my hand, and we ran towards the exit. Whole time he was shielding me by his body. We came towards the vehicle in which we came, and he started driving like crazy. I saw a huge vehicle ahead of us. I hope it does contain the girls. Rest of the men and that girl stayed back, I don't know why. I pray that they get back safe and unharmed, thought now I wonder who is more dangerous, one who helped me or one from whom we ran away.

I peeked at Vincent and my heart skipped a beat. This is what I am scared of. I am scared of how my heart is reacting to his presence. Why was I getting attracted to him? The way we met and the way I feel for him feels is so right, as if we were destined to meet and fated for life, yet it was so wrong. I was scared of my feelings. In this short time, he felt close as if there were an unbreakable invisible bond between us. He came like a storm in my life and whisked me away to his home. He endured all my tantrums, even his friends and family tolerated my childishness. They even helped me in bringing these girls back, risking their lives. Why? I was no one to them, to him. Whenever he touched me my whole body was lit on fire, my breathing gets heavy, my heart starts thumping with happiness and my brain gets fizzy. The way he talked to me this morning...it felt like even he is attracted to me. The way he held my face and those green orbs gazed in mine, it touched my soul and shook me to the core. When he tackled me to the ground, his hand was firm yet caring. He had engulfed me in his warmth and when he leaned in I felt he was going to kiss me. But why, why will a boy like him so handsome and rich and sophisticated will like someone like me...

I can't let my heart go crazy like this, I can't allow myself to feel for him. That's why I was being rude and harsh to him, but now I need to get away. Good, we found the girls. We will go back today itself. Away from him, where I belong. I don't belong here, or with him.

I just can't. I am not allowed.

———————————

Hey everyone,An Early update...

This is the very first point of view of Aroha. Do let me know what you think about it. I would be interested in knowing your thoughts.

I really hope you enjoy reading this chapter. And if you do then Please Vote, comment and share

Follow me here and on instagram (curiouswords27)

Her territory

I pulled the car with a jerk some distance away from the pack house. Jia was standing at the door with her hands on her hips. I saw Jake pulling over the trailer right beside me. He got down and so did I. We are dead for sure. The drama back there will be nothing compared to this one, for sure.

"We are screwed, isn't it?" He said, looking at Jia

"Royally screwed. What do we tell her?" We need to give the same answers if we need to live.

"We followed Alpha's order?" Jake suggested.

"Ya... that's quite reasonable." We did actually follow Alpha's orders.

Aroha came and stood beside me with a frown on her face and Rick too got down, just then another car pulled up near us. it contained the rest of our team, all of them came out, and I was relieved that everyone was ok. No injuries on our end, But when lastly Hunter came out and closed the door, I furrowed my brows. Where is the Alpha?

Jia came rushing towards us with her little army.

"Where is Richard?" She asked no one in particular.

"Ummm..." I tried, but I clearly had no idea. When bullets started firing, I grabbed Aroha's hand and sprinted towards the exit not thinking about anyone and anything but my mate's safety.

"Where is your Alpha? Vinci?... Jake?" Her eyes landed on us with accusation. Both of us held our head low.

"Luna, Alpha stayed back..." Dal tried to explain, but Jia cut him off midway

"You all came back, leaving him alone?"

"No...he asked us to leave as he wanted to meet..." Dal kept looking at me as if asking for help.

"Non of you thought of staying back with him"

"We ...I.."

"What's happening here?" Alpha came and stood beside Jia as if nothing happened. How did he come?

"How did you..." Jia questioned but stopped. I think they are mind linking.

"I had to speak with the authorities and complete all their documentation." He explained. I side glanced at Aroha and her mouth was wide open, of course wondering how Alpha landed here. She then looked at me, but I instantly looked away, not wanting to explain her.

"Can we check the girls, please. " She finally said after a few seconds of silence.

I translated her wish.

"Ya sure." Alpha gestured her to follow him.All of us went and stood behind Rick, who was opening the trailer door. As soon as the door opened, we heard shrieks of all the girls.

Oh! my Goddess. What have they done to them? They were a crying mess. They were cramped up together in the far corner, hugging each other and they smelled fear and anguish.

Aroha climbed and started soothing them with her words. Next, Jia too got in to help, girls were in a panic and were shattered.Two girls hugged Aroha and cried.

"We should take them side and let our in-house doctor tend them." Alpha Richard suggested. Aroha still had the ear pods on so she knew what he told.

"No it we would be better if we get them home as soon as possible." She said not looking at us,

"They need medical help and some food..." I tried to make her stay long.

"We should leave." She said so firmly that non of us could argue further.

"She wants to leave right away." I translated for others.

"Ok"

"Get Dr Tonia along with us and Dal please get something to eat from the kitchen." Alpha instructed everyone.

Soon we were on our way to her tribe. She was sitting in front of trailer with Rich driving it and the rest of us were inside with the girls. I and Bro sat at a further distance as Jia and Dr. Tonia sat with them.

I felt trailer halting in the middle of nowhere, and with that, my heart stopped beating. I was not ready to leave her. My mind was fogged with numerous thoughts. How do I tell her what she is to me, how I can't survive without her.

Rick opened the door and all of us to came out.

"Myself, Vince and Luna will accompany them, rest of you stay here."
Alpha announced as we all had gathered on the ground. We started walking
behind Aroha on a small trail, and soon a community came into view. Hut
were scattered around and people were going about their daily activities.
As soon as they saw us, there was an uproar among them, families of girls
came running towards us and started hugging their daughters and cried
with happy tears.

A man came running and hugged Aroha as if his life depended on it. My
blood boiled with rage. How dare he touch my mate. I was about to drag
him away, but Jia stopped me by grabbing my fisted hand.

"He must be the brother" Jia reasoned.

"This doesn't look like brotherly" I gritted.

"Vinci we want to avoid creating a scene here." Bro ordered.

I looked at them and again my eyes moved to Aroha, that guy had auda-
ciously cupped her face and had joined their foreheads. He was mumbling
something, to which she was nodding her head. My hand fisted, and my
jaws clenched even Al was in full attention, ready to attack. Here I was
boiling on rage and bro was concerned about not creating a scene.

Hell with it. I will just rip him apart. I had just moved when an elderly man
came and engulfed Aroha in his arms.

"Taku tamahine toa. Ka whakahīhī ahau ki a koe" he said lovingly

(My brave daughter. I am proud of you.)

He seemsmed leader of this tribe as all others bowed to him.

Aroha started explaining to him everything, gesturing her hands at us. Her
father came to us and extended his hand.

"Myself Rangi, I extend my hearty gratitude for helping my daughter in rescuing all the girls. My people and I will be thankful to you for all our lives." That man spoke in English. We were astonished, but then bro extended his arm and introduced us.

"Richard Stanford. My brother Vincent and my wife Jia. I consider it my duty to fight injustice, and what these girls faced was unbelievable." He replied.

"My people want you all to stay back, so they could express their gratitude." He said, gesturing towards his people.

"It's not needed seriously..." Bro said.

"Tēnā koa. Please we insist"

"We will stay" I replied quickly. I wanted to talk to Aroha before leaving.

"Let me introduce everyone here. This is Maugham my head advisor and This is Tane Maugham 's son and Aroha's fiancé..."

Look who updated after such a long time....

Hope you enjoy read.

Heartless Humans

My ears were ringing with the word 'Fiancé'. Every sound was wiped away, and a constant buzz had engulfed me. This can't be true, my mate can't have a fiancé. She is mine, JUST MINE. How can she love someone other than me? She is betrothed to me by the moon goddess. I don't know. When I started vibrating and Al started surfacing, but I was pulled into the woods by Derek. (Derek is Alpha Richard's wolf)

"Calm down." He hollered.

Al was ready to kill. He wanted his mate, he was not concerned about human customs, not bothered to wipe off the whole tribe.

"I want mate. She is mine. MINE" Al growled, I was unable to take control from him as I was so hurt. Derek had to pin Al by the tree to stop him from claiming our mate.

"She is yours. Relax. We will figure this out. You need to Calm down. We can't show ourselves to humans." Derek reasoned, but Al was in no condition to hear. He was trashing to get out of Derek's hold.

"ALDRICH STOP" Derek commanded in his Alpha tone that made Al to stop getting out of control, he stood still and bowed to his Alpha.

"Bring Vinci back." Richard commanded this time in a calm voice.. When I opened my eyes, I saw bro staring at me skeptically.

"Are you okay?" He asked, patting my back. I just nodded as I was exhausted fighting with Derek. I was breathing heavily and tried to regain my composure. I glanced around and found that we were surrounded by thick forest. We must be deep in the woods. After a few minutes, we went back. Jia gave me a tight lipped smile.

I felt so hurt that my heart felt numb. I never imagined that I would be in such a situation. Aroha has become the epicenter of my survival from the moment she stepped into my life, but I was not anything to her. My mate's heart holds some other man, and that left a constant pang in my heart.

We were sitting at the dinner table, with me sitting right in front of Aloha. Her so-called Fiancé was sitting next to her, holding her hand and feeding her from his plate. I was clenched my fist and gulped my rage. My brain was buzzing from contact fight with Al, who wanted to take control over me again. All this while I kept staring at Aroha who was very much aware of my eyes on her because she kept stealing glances at me and her cheeks were flushed.

I can easily kidnap her and take her to our world. No one will ever find her, but I would rather not use force. I want her heart and her willingness to spend her life with me after knowing everything. I thought we had some strings attached while being on that mission, as if she felt our bond. Maybe I was wrong, all of that was just in my head perhaps, she never felt anything. Humans don't feel our bond, they are selfish, insensitive...

"I think we should leave. Thanks again for your hospitality Leader Rangi" Bro stood up from the table and so did Jia. I followed their suit. My food was untouched. Aroha noticed it and glanced at me. I started at her, holding our eyes together. I wanted to talk to her, shake her up and get some answers out of her. I felt cheated, betrayed and blamed her for breaking my heart. But then again, she is just a human, a heartless human who is unaware of the sacred bond Moon goddess has blessed her with.

We moved to our car. Bro had already told the rest of our team to leave. Jia was holding my hand, squeezing them to show her support. I felt defeated and broke on leaving my mate behind, but still, I gave her a small smile. Bro was walking ahead of us, we reached the car and I opened the car door and slammed it close, gaining the attention of Jia and Bro.

"This is so unbelievable" I fumed, losing all piled up resilience.

"Vinci.." Jia started, but I continued.

"Why? Why can't she love me? What do I do now? Should I.... should I re.. reject her...?"

"Vincent Stanford, don't you dare say such words. She is your mate for a reason. Have faith in the Moon goddess. Aroha will be with you. You will have your mate...I, Alpha Richard Stanford, will make sure of it." Bro hollered.

"Now get in the damn car, we are leav..."

"Vincent" all of us turned to the source of the voice and there stood my mate. Her eyes were on me trying to say something, and it was the first time she had called my name.

I slowly walked towards her, getting very close. What does she want now, I wondered.

"Can you both, please leave us alone" I requested Jia and Alpha. Without much thought or delay, they climbed in the car and drove away.

I pinned her to the nearby tree and buried my head in the nook of her neck. She started breathing heavily, her heart started beating fast, I could hear it.

"Do you love him?" I mumbled, still being in that position. Her scent calmed me.

"I whakarerea koe i konei!" She said, but I didn't understand anything.

(They just left you here!)

"You are my mate, how do I tell youthis?" I moved up and caressed her cheeks.

"E mohio ana ahau kare koe e marama ki ahau engari ko ahau....Ki taku whakaaro kei te pai ahau ki a koe. He tino rerekee, kare e mohio ki a maua engari kare e taea e au" she said something.

(I know you can't understand me, but I....I think I like you. It's so weird, we hardly know each other, but I can't help it.)

"Don't you feel our bond. Don't you feel anything for me?" I cupped both her cheeks and tried desperately to make her understand.

"Ko te tikanga o to tatou iwi me moe au i a Tane...e te Atua kei te aha ahau"This Tane again. I hate when she takes his name. I want to kill him.

(I... It's our tribe's custom. I have to marry Tane...oh God what am I doing)

"Come with me, please. I can't survive without you" I almost pleaded.

"He he tenei. Kore rawa ahau i haere mai i muri i a koe. Ka pouri ahau. Kare au e mohio he aha taku i whakaaro ai? Ka pouri ahau, ka pouri ahau" she pushed me a bit and started walking away from me, finally vanishing behind the trees and back to her tribe and back to her Tane. Al growled.

(This is wrong. I should have never come after you. I am sorry. I don't know, what was I thinking? I am sorry, I am so sorry)

"Aroha...Arohaaa...this is not over, Aroha. I am coming back for you. I will be back soon to take you with me." I yelled behind her and finally gave control to Al.

————

Hey Readers.

I had not updated since long. Sorry for that. Hope you are still connected to the story.

Thanks a lot. Please follow, vote and comment.

Three days

- -

A roha's pov

She was thinking in her language, but I translated it.

I just can't believe what I did. Why? Why Aroha? Why did you go behind him? What will he think now. Why you show your interest in him. Why give him false hope? And why give false hope to yourself.

I am betrothed to Tane I can't think of anyone else. I just can't. I don't love him, but it was decided when I was born that we both will be married. My father is the head of our tribe, his son would be the ideal person to get his position, but then I was born a girl child. My mom passed away giving birth to me, so my father didn't get a chance to get a son. As per the custom, I have to marry the son of our head advisor and if I deny, then he can challenge my father for the position.

The challenge is very cruel, it ends with the death of one of the participants. My father is old and no match to Tane of course, he will lose and will be killed by Tane and I...I will be forced to be marrying him. So the sensible thing was to agree for this union.

I was okay with Tane. He was not that bad. Until now that is. After meeting Vincent, I somehow don't like Tane, I hate it when he touches me...

"taku kotiro" I heard Tane's voice. I hate it when he calls me that. I am not his.

(My girl)He came to my room and sat beside me on the bed.

"I tino mihi ahau ki a koe. I wehi koe i ahau. Kaua e pena ano"

(I missed you so much. You scared me. Don't do that ever again) he said, taking me in his arms. I just stayed silent. What do I tell him? That I missed him when I didn't.

Kei hea koe kua ngaro?

(Where are you lost?) he asked, moving away. I shake my head, telling nothing happened.

"E hiahia ana ahau ki te whakaatu ki a koe i tetahi mea"

(I want to show you something) he took my hand and got up, pulling me along.I was exhausted mentally and physically. All the action and stress had drained my energy, and constant thinking about Vincent made my head ache. I wanted to rest and sleep, waking to new tomorrow where everything will be how it was before our girls went missing, and before I met him. I was already dark outside. We soon reached in front of a house. I know this place, and I dreaded going inside.

This is the place where we will be living after getting married. Tane had started building this house long back, and it was still incomplete when I went out for the mission. But it was done and Tane had done an excellent work on it. It is our custom that man build house for their future wives.

It's a beautiful house with sloping roof covered with hay and walls painted in white and red color. The interior was spacious, the walls were decorated with artwork

"Kei te pehea? He pai ki a koe?"

(How is it? You like it?) We were inside a beautiful house, but it scared me. This is my future home, where I will form a family with Tane. WITH TANE and not...

I looked at Tane as he beamed with pride, waiting egarly for my response. I don't intend to hurt his feelings, he is not at fault here. It's my fault that I let someone enter my heart when I am already promised to someone.

"He mea whakamiharo ... ataahua"

(It's amazing... beautiful) I smiled facing him

"Kei te tino koa ahau i pai ki a koe. Ka mahia e au etahi taonga me tetahi moenga i roto i nga ra torutoru, ka hoko ano i etahi taputapu kihini."

(I am so happy you liked it. I will make some furniture and a bed in few days, also buy some kitchen utensils.) He said, looking around as if picturing their location.

He came forward and hugged me, taking me a back. He pulled back after a few seconds and cupped my face, glancing at my lips. His stare made me uncomfortable. He leaned in to kiss, and my heart ached. I don't want him to touch me this way, it felt wrong and disgusting. I pushed him out of impulse. He stumbled back at me and glared at me. I saw him clenching his jaws.

"Ka huri koe i ahau i nga wa katoa"(You always turn me down) he sheathed holding my atm in a tight grip

"Ko ahau... pouri a Tane engari kua ngenge ahau i muri i nga mea katoa i puta i tenei ra"(I am...sorry Tane but I am tired after everything that happened today)

"E toru nga ra e toru noa nga ra ka waiho koe hei wahine maku. Kia kite koe me pehea e huri ai koe i ahau i muri i tera."(Three days, just three days and then you will be my wife. Let's see how you turn me down after that.) He threatened and pushed me, leaving me alone in the empty house.

Three days!

Not without my mate

Vincent 's pov

Three days, 3 fu*king days, 8 hours, 37 minutes and 11 seconds...12. the exact time I have not seen my mate. It's driving me crazy. Every second feels like a heavy stone on my heart. I can't take this anymore. I want my mate right now and I am going to do that right now no matter what. I don't care if her people are enraged or know about our existence. To hell with it. I need to think of some plan. It's now or never. I was not feeling good about something. It felt like I was losing her by every passing second.

"This is it." I got up and slammed my hands on the desk with determination.

"What is it?" Dal asked, astonished at my sudden outburst. All of us were sitting in my study. Dal and Hunter were playing video games and Wayne was busy on his mobile. All their eyes were on me, waiting for the response.

"I refuse to spend one more day without my mate. I have decided." Hunter raised his brows.

"I am going back to their tribe land and getting my mate where she belongs, that is with me." I declared, expecting a positive response but all I got was silence.

"Who is coming with me?" I probed them further, still no word for them. They just kept staring at me like fools.

"Like to go and kidnap her?" Hunter asked.

"Yeah...something like that." I replied with positivity. Call it anything. I am just focusing on getting her here before she gets married to that idiot.

"Nah...we are good." Dal and Hunter got back to playing without second thought. I looked at Wayne the most sensible one but bloody fu*cker went back to his mobile as if no questions were asked.

"Wow, some friends I have got" I scoffed. I thought they would jump on the idea and will be my support for the mission.

"Guess I am doing this alone then." I huffed. They are not responding at all as if I don't exist.

"What are you doing alone?" Jia came to my study and asked.

"Going on a death mission." Hunter replied with his eyes still in the game. I just rolled my eyes at that.

"What does that mean?" She questioned

"I am going to get Aroha back"

"WHAT."

"yes. I am going even if no one wants to come with me. I will go alone. Something is not right, I just feel it. The restlessness and anxiety. I think they are her emotions. I have to go and get her before it's too late. I don't care even if I have to fight her whole tribe." I was having everyone's attention now. They were looking at me with pity.

"Okay, let's go" Jia broke the silence. I was so astonished to hear it.

You ...are coming with me?

"Of course I am coming with you. I can't let you go all alone over there." she replied as a matter of fact. I was so overwhelmed that I went and hugged her, stumbling her in the process. She is my true friend and I love her.

"I love you." I jested. She giggled at my response.

"Luna, What about Alpha? He will never approve of it" Wayne pointed out.

"We will worry about that later. For now, let's go and get your mate." Jia said.

After Jia gave her support, my friends decided to come along. We asked Hunter to say back so he can keep an eye on Alpha. We also asked Brittany to take care of both the kids.

We rushed towards the parking lot without wasting time. Just as we were about the open the car door and get in, we smelled him.

"Where are you all going?" Alpha asked behind us. Oh! Goddess, here goes our plan. I and Jia turned to face him.

'What now?' I mindlinked Jia.

'I will handle him, don't worry.' She replied and gave her best smile to her mate.

"Sweetheart" she went and hugged him. "I was getting so bored and you never have time for me. so I asked these guys to take me for a drive." She said with a pout. Alpha furrowed his brows. He definitely found something fishy. Jia was overdoing it. She is never so sweet to him.

"What are you all up to?" He asked suspiciously looking at all of us one by one

"Nothing...nothing..."she replied too quickly.

Just then we heard growling and paws hitting the ground. As if 2 to 3 of them were coming running to us and then I was hit by that smell. Sandalwood. My mate's smell, next I saw her emerging from the bushes and running towards me. I went forward to hold her.

"Wuruhi..." she mumbled and fainted in my arms.

(Wolves)

Aroha yes Vincent

- -

V incent 's pov

I just could not believe what I was seeing in front of me.

Aroha is sleeping on my bed in some boho kind of bridal attire, me holding her hand and gawking at her.

Just when I was going to get her, she came running towards me. patrolling Wolves said that they saw her roaming around the forest looking for something. They had to chase her here so that she could reach us. She got scared of wolves chasing after her and fainted as soon as she saw me. If she got scared of wolves then how am I supposed to tell her about us without her running away. But the main question is why she is here? Did those girls get kidnapped again? But why will she come to us for help? She has her whole tribe for that. Did she...no...no that's not possible right? She didn't run away from her wedding to Tane because she has feelings for me...is it possible?

"Why are you staring at her like that?" Jia nudged me with her elbow.

"Is she really here or am I dreaming? Can you pinch me?" She pinched with all her might on my arm.

"Aahhhh. What the hel..." I yelled but she stopped me

"Shhh! You will wake her up." She whispered.

"Shouldn't she wake up by now? it's been an hour..." I inquired.

"Then start shouting. Maybe she will wake up by hearing your voice." She suggested and at that moment Aroha stirred a bit. I immediately placed her hand on the bed not wanting her to get agitated. I glared at Jia and she shrugged it off.

Aroha tried to open her eyes and blinked them to adjust to the light. She then looked here and there taking in her surroundings I suppose. All of us were looking at her, ready for her to explode any time. I was a bit scared but as her eyes landed on me she got up and hugged me.

I was baffled, I never ever thought that she would hug me like her life depended on it.

"He wuruhi... Wuruhi, he tini... I tino mataku ahau. I whakaaro ahau ka taea e au te haere mai ki konei kaore he raru engari kua ngaro ahau kaore au i mohio ki hea ka haere, katahi ka kite au i nga wuruhi..."

(There were wolves. Wolves, so many. I was so scared. I thought I would be able to come here without any problem but I got lost and didn't know where to go and...and then I saw wolves...they...they started chasing me...I was so scared...)

She started crying in my arms. I didn't know what she was saying but was able to understand that she was scared. I could feel it.

'She is scared of wolves...what an irony' Al jabbed making me nervous but I pushed that feeling aside and caressed Aroha's hair.

"It's ok, you are safe now. Those wolves will never harm you. They wouldn't dare and in any way wolves don't eat humans." I chuckled to relax her.

"I whakaaro ahau e kore ahau e kite i a koe ka mate i mua i te tutakitanga... i mua i taku korerotanga ki a koe mo aku karekau...Ka oma ahau i toku whare. Kare au i pirangi ki te marena ia Tane no reira ka oma ahau. I tino mataku ahau ka taea e au te whakaaro i taku oranga me Tane." She sniffed

(I thought I would never see you again and die before we could meet...before I could tell you about my feelings...I ran away from my house. I didn't want to marry Tane so I ran away. I was so scared I could imagine my life with Tane.)

Okay, this is the second time I heard 'Tane,' and I don't like it. I pulled her away from me with my hands on her shoulders

"Tane? What about Tane?" I raised my brows for her to ask what she was talking about Tane.

"Kare au e pirangi ki te marena ia Tane I...I pai ahau ki a koe...A...Aroha no ...Tane" she stuttered. Wait a minute. Did she speak English? 'Aroha no Tane' means she doesn't want him. right? Did she learn to speak English from her dad? For me?

(I don't want to marry Tane I ...I like you.)

"What?" I looked deep in her eyes and asked again.

"Aroha no Tane...Aroha...y..yes ...Vincent..." she mumbled and kept her head low, shying.

Oh goddess, does she mean what I am thinking? 'Aroha yes Vincent'. She likes me and she said yes to me. oh my. I just hope that's what she is saying.

I am feeling so happy and wondering if this is actually happening with me? I was just stupidly staring at her.

She looked up in my eyes with hesitation and doubt.

"Vincent...no... Aroha?" She choked.

"What? no...no... ofcourse I like you. You are my mate. In Fact I love you. I was going to come and get you...we were just leaving when you turned up. I am so happy. You just can't imagine...

"Is it?" Bro asked? With his hands folded on his chest. I had just forgotten that Bro, Jia and my friends were in the same room.

I shifted my focus back on Aroha who was frowning. She must have not understood anything. So I tried again

"Vincent yes Aroha. A big yes." I spread my arms to show her how much I like her. She gave me a radiant smile but tensed up again.

"Me hoki ano tatou. Me whawhai koe ki a Tane kia noho koe hei upoko mo toku iwi, kei patua e ratou toku matua." She said in a worried tone.

(We need to go back again. You need to fight Tane and be the head of my tribe or else they will kill my father.)

Again Tane! I got up from my place and brought the earpods. I need to understand what she is saying.

"Can you repeat what you said earlier?" I requested after activating mine and her earpods.

"Me whawhai koe ki a Tane kia ora ai taku matua"

"You have to fight Tane and save my father," she pleaded.

WHAT!

Hey everyone, hope you enjoy reading.

Do follow if you like the story and want to read further.

Thank

Votes and comments please.

Happiness

Vincent 's pov

"So you ran away from your wedding?" Alpha Richard asked Aro ha.We were all sitting in my room and wanted to know all the details of Aroha's escape.

"Y..Yes" she replied in English. She has learnt few words and tries her best to communicate with them

"That's brave of you" He concluded.

"T ..Thank" she gave a tight lipped smile to him.

"Why?" He probed further.

"Aroha..no...Tane ..." she started but Bro stopped her.

"Ya we got it Aroha no Tane but Aroha yes Vinci we get that loud and clear but what made you do it?" Bro rolled his eyes. I glared at him. I like hearing her say 'Aroha yes Vincent' . It sounds so romantic and more romantic was her effort to learn English for me.

"Umm...Aroha...

"Just a sec. Please tell us in your language." Bro pinched his bridge of nose getting frustrated.

"Aroha English learn" she said sternly glaring at Bro.

"Goddess knows who taught her" he mumbled, rolling his eyes, making me furious.

"Vinci, can you connect these earpods to some speaker so we all can understand her?" He asked me and I squinted my eyes at him. My mate was trying her best to communicate with us. She even went ahead and learnt the language.

"What?" He shrugged as if it was her faultI sighed and got up to connect my earpods to Alexa

"Aroha you can tell us in your language" I requested softly

She gave me a tight lipped smile and nodded

"So let me start from the start." She said it in her language and just then Alexa translated it into English in her very annoying voice. This process was not ideal but we can't help it.

Alexa repeated her every sentence.

"It's my tribe's custom that the Tribe head's daughter will marry Tribe advisor 's son and pass on the position to him if there is no son in the picture. So I was betrothed to Tane since I was born as my mother died giving birth to me."

"If ...if I oppose this union then Tane will challenge my father for the position. It's a brutal duel which ends with the death of any of them."

"Tane is our best warrior. He is very strong. My father is no match for him. He will kill him easily. I...I don't know what to do...can ...can you please save my father." She pleaded.

I know where this is going. I am just waiting for her to say the words.

"And how do we save him?" I asked, fully aware of what was coming my way.

"Someone has to fight Tane" she spoke very slowly

"And by someone you mean Vinci right?" Bro probed and Aroha looked at me. She gave a small nod and diverted her eyes on the floor. She was on the verge of tears and it was affecting me. I can fight the whole world for her.

"I am sorry I am dragging you in this mess but I can't marry Tane...not after...after meeting you. I don't understand or can't pinpoint what it is but it feels as if we have some eternal bond... As if we are meant to be ...and I didn't want to give myself away to some egocentric stubborn guy before exploring our bond." She explained looking deep in my eyes

My heart fluttered at her words.

"Tane is a very aggressive and strong guy. He has been training for years. He is 27 years old. He won't give up easily. It's his dream to be head of the tribe" she explained

"I will fight him." I announced. No matter how strong that Tane might be, he can't beat a werewolf.

"No you are not getting it. You can't just go and fight him. You need to train first. You are no match to him. And also you are very young." She panicked but was shocked when everyone in the room laughed.

Ouch! That hit hard.

"I am eighteen, I can fight him, don't worry." I assured her. I am a warrior, that too trained by the best. I am confident that I can defeat him. I don't intend on killing him nor want to be head of her tribe. This will just be just for claiming my mate. Aroha is mine and no Tane can come in between.

"But..." she tried to say something but bro held his palm at her.

"We will go tomorrow, and trust me Tane will be running for his life." He smirked and slapped my back as he moved towards the door and the rest of everyone followed him out. It was just me and Aroha now in the room. We may have confessed our feelings for eachother but still we are a bit strangers. We hardly know each other. Aroha went and sat on the bed avoiding looking at me although she had a hint of a shy smile on her lips. I went and sat next to her letting the fact sink in that she is actually here with me, that she came to me and that she has feelings for me.

"I am so happy that you are here with me and you thought of giving us a chance." She nodded and smiled brightly, still avoiding my eyes. This Aroha is so different from the previous one. I chuckled at the thought which made her look at me with a frown.

"I didn't know you could be so timid. I like the previous Aroha more." I told. She glared at me, turning her face towards me. I cupped her face in my palms, she gasped closing her eyes. I was so mesmerized with her beauty that I can spend my whole life just gazing at her.

When she opened her eyes they were moist and held fear in them.

"I am worried for you and my father...Tane..."

"Shh...Trust me everything will be alright." I tried to hug her but she placed her palms on my chest.

"Umm...." She wanted to say something. I raised my brows at her

"I am 21 years old. I am older than you" she confessed.

"It doesn't matter" I laughed taker her in my arms.

Hey everyone, hope you are enjoying the story so far.

Please comment you views on the storyline.

And please vote and follow me here and on Instagram.

Guilt

T ane

Aroha's pov

This guilt is eating me. I am doing this again, making him face danger for me. I just can't understand myself at times. He is going to fight for me, me who he has met just briefly. We hardly know each other irrespective of the strong bond that pulls us together. What is this bond? Why is it so strong? I left my father, my people, my fiance on my wedding day for him? And he is no different, he is ready to go face any danger for me. Now he is going to fight Tane who is twice his age and strength. Oh Goddess what was I thinking? Aroha, how can you be so cruel? He is just eighteen, even younger than you. You are going to hell for this.

I still have my suspicions, something is different about him, about all these people. They are extremely strong, fast and handsome. I mean just look at Vincent, he is breathtakingly gorgeous. His eyes...those dark green orbs are like some mysterious forest. I feel like they are calling me and as if I belong there. Why the hell does he like me of all people? Someone he can't even communicate with. I didn't know my father knew how to speak English. It was a shock for me. So I forced him to teach me. I wanted to learn Vincent 's language so that we could communicate freely without the help of any device but I hardly got any time to learn it properly. I still want to learn it. If we have a future together then I should be able to understand the language and I will learn it. And there is this bond, again it's so not natural. The pull, affection and love...ya love, I know it's a heavy word but somehow what I feel for him is not ordinary. I despised the thought of being with Tane, thought of him touching me. I felt as if I were cheating on Vincent, as if I was betraying him. There is something beyond what meets the eyes. I need to ask him. But whatever it may be. My heart belongs to him forever.

"Hey where are you lost?" Vincent nudged me with his shoulder breaking my train of thoughts. Both of us were wearing that device in our ears which translates. We were going to my tribe in a car which Richard was driving. Jia was sitting beside him. Me and Vincent were sitting at the back. During the whole ride everyone was silent, lost in their own thoughts. Before I could answer him. Richard's voice reached me, making me panic.

"We are here." He stopped the car.

I wanted to turn around and run back to safety. Back to their place where Vincent won't need to face Tane and fight him but my father's life was at stake. I couldn't disregard that fact.

Everyone got down but my legs were frozen. How do I face my people, my father, they will judge me and accuse me for bringing this on them. And Tane, he will hate me and will be furious for leaving him alone standing at the altar. He will take out all his anger on Vincent.

'What's wrong?" Vincent asked peeping back in the car with his one arm on the bonet

"I am scared," I mumbled. He sat back inside and faced me

"Do you trust me?" He raised his brows in question.

"I don't trust Tane. He is a beast and he gets very violent when challenged. He will ... he will try every possible way to kill you ... I don't know how to face this..."

"Hey you have me and it's not easy to kill me alright. No Tane can ever harm me.Please have faith in me. You may not believe it but I am no less than a beast myself." He chuckled. I still feel he is not getting the seriousness of the situation

"Come let's go."His determination gave me faith. Somehow Vincent was very confident and firm that he would defeat Tane

Okay let's do this. There is no going back now. I nodded and we both came out of the car. As we started walking through the trees. Richard stopped on his track, raising his hand to make us all stop.

"Do you smell it?" He asked Vincent. What smell is he talking about?

"The kidnapers? What are they doing here? Are they planning something again?"

Kidnapers? What kidnapers?How do they know they are here? I can't see anyone around us... I told you these brothers are not normal.

"I smell him too...what is he doing with them?" Vincent gritted his teeth and got furious. What are they talking about? They are doing it again, talking with their eyes...they just stare at each other and their expressions keep changing. I have to learn this too.

We moved a bit forward around the turn and then I saw a few men talking with each other. It looked more like they were arguing rather than talking. I recognised one of them from our tribe as he was wearing our tribal clothes and the other two were wearing city clothes.

"You heard that?" Richard asked Vincent, getting angry. Don't tell me these brothers could hear what they were speaking because that's impossible. Those men were quite far from us. How could they hear what they were speaking?

"Bloody bastard. I knew he was not a good fellow." Vincent snarled. What just happened. Why are they so furious?

"Can anyone please tell me what's happening?" I inquired getting annoyed

"Your Tane helped in kidnapping the girls, he is their friend. Good you ran away" Richard said sarcastically.

Hey everyone, hope you enjoy reading this chapter.

Please vote, comment and Follow.Your feedback is much needed.

And sorry for late update.

Traitors

- -

J ia 's pov

I could not believe it. How could he sell girls of his own tribe? That Tane was a bloody traitor just like Tyler. Tane. Tyler. Traitor. Has ' T ' got anything to do with traitors? I will never trust anyone whose name starts with 'T' from now on. These traitors should not be shown any mercy, they should be killed because they never learn. Those who can cheat their own people cannot be forgiven. They are leeches that suck faith and trust out of us.

I feel sorry for Aroha and her people. They are being deceived by their future leader. It's horrifying what he will do once he becomes their head. Girls won't be safe under his rule. I hope Vinci will finish him and if not I will do the honors. I looked at Aroha. She looks devastated. Good she ran away from her marriage to that traitor. I placed my hand on her shoulder to show her support. We will always have her back, she is family now.

"I am so sorry you had to face betrayal. It hurts more than anything. I can understand." I sympathized with her. I know she will understand me as she was wearing the earpods. She gave an assuring smile.

"I no guilt kill him." She said with determination. As I didn't have the translation ear pods she replied in English. I got the feeling behind her words.

"She is saying that..." Vinci tried to explain me what Aroha said in her english attempt, but I stopped him

"I got it, lover boy." I rolled my eyes at him just to annoy him.

"Lover boy? Me? Have you seen bro around you. " he sassed giving me a sly smirk.

"Whatever" I grunted and started walking toward my mate. My baby was tensed, he was walking ahead of us looking in all directions. I interlinked our fingers.

"Relax, everything will be okay." I mindlinked him. He looked at me with those green orbs that could see through my soul. My breath got hitched, he can still give me flutter by just looking at me.

"I don't trust Tane, he could harm Vinci." He replied with worry.

"Tane can't do anything when we both are here. No one can lay their fingers on Vinci." I assured him. Vinci is our life we love just as we love Danial and Damien.

He nodded as we entered the tribe, people started noticing us and there were murmurs all around us. I don't know what they are saying but they don't seem happy. Soon murmurs turned into yells. We surrounded Aroha from all sides. They were targeting their hate towards her.

"Me pehea koe, e te kotiro whakama."

(How could you, you shameless girl.)

"uwha whakama"

(Shameless bitch)

"Kei te mohio ano koe ki nga mahi i mahia e koe?"

(Do you even know what you have done?)

"Me poutoa koe"

(You should be beheaded.)

"Nau i mea kia whakama to papa"

(You brought shame on your father)

Aroha was getting nervous with all the comments. Vinci understood what they were saying as he pulled her near him wrapping his arm around her shoulders.

"Ahh, kei konei koe. I tatari ahau mo koe"

(Ahh, here you are. I was waiting for you) came a strong venomous voice ahead of us. My head snapped in his direction and there he was, Traitor glaring at Aroha.

————

A short chapter, just a filler. Hope you enjoy it. It's in Jia 's pov.

Guys, please give some feedback. I am writing the story without any response and so it doesn't excite me to write next chapter.

Please vote and comment so I get excited to write further and updates will be earlier.

I don't usually ask my readers to follow me but if you like my work then please vote comment and Follow. It's free.

Thanks in advance.

Challenge

V incent 's pov

"Ahh, kei konei koe. I tatari ahau mo koe"

(Ahh, here you are. I was waiting for you)

Spoke the bastard, glaring at Aroha. His voice and his eyes extruded venom. He is making Aroha a culprit whereas he is nothing less than a cold blooded criminal.

My blood was boiling with rage. He had the audacity to humiliate and degrade Aroha in front of all people when he should be castrated and hanged to death

"Inaianei kei konei koe me o hoa aroha e whakaatu ana i te kanohi whakama ki a koe, me korero e ahau ki a koe mo nga mea i tupu tata nei i a koe e hora ana i ou waewae mo ratou"

(Now that you are here with your lovers showing you shameful faces, let me update you on the recent events that happened while you were spreading your legs for them) I will bloody kill him without any mercy.

"Me te mea kei a koe te tika ki te whakapae i ahau. Tukua ahau..."

(As if you have any right to accuse me. Let me...) Aroha yelled but I stopped her to say anything about our discovery. I don't want anyone to think we are blaming him just to save us, first I will defeat him and then we can tell everyone the truth.

"No....not know..." I stopped her. She looked at me with a frown.

"He aha te mea i tupu? karekau he mea hei korero? Haere mai...whakapae mai kia ora koe..."

(What happened? you don't have anything to say? Come on...accuse me to save yourself...) see what I was referring to? He did just that. When Aroha didn't respond he continued.

"Kaati, me haere tonu ahau ki nga korero hou...he aha to whakaaro...ka tatari ahau ki a koe i te tuahu, ka tirotiro i oku kanohi mo taku mate, ka pouri i te mea kua mahue taku aroha..."

"Well then, let me continue with the updates...what you thought...I would wait for you at the altar, browling my eyes for my loss, go into depression because my love left me..." he chuckled mocking Aroha.

"Karekau he hoa aroha, kua marenatia ahau i tera ra. Kei te hiahia koe ki te whakatau i taku wahine? Ka koa koe ki te whakatau ia ia."

(No sweetheart, I got married as I was supposed to on that day. Want to meet my wife? You will be pleased to meet her.) He is certified sick the way he was laughing.

He was alone speaking among the whole tribe gathered around us.

"Drew, e kore e taea e koe te kawe mai taku wahine ki konei? Kia tupato, he po kino rawa tana po."

((Drew, can you please bring my wife here? Be careful, she had a very rough night.) Tane said to the person standing behind him. That Drew fellow nodded and left. Soon he returned dragging a girl with him. This bastard was the same as his boss. Ruthless. He dropped the girl at Tane's feet. She was sobbing silently with her head held low and made no attempt to stand. She looked lost and defeated. Tane crouched down to her level and held her jaw in a tight grip making her face us.

"E hoa aroha, tirohia ko wai kei konei ki te whakatau i a koe"

(Sweetheart, see who's here to meet you) Tane gritted.

Aroha grasped recognising the girl "Pania"

she whispered and ran towards her. I tried to stop her but she was gone before I could hold her back. She pushed Tane to free Pania from his grip and hugged the girl. Pania started crying uncontrollably and hugged Aroha tightly. Poor girl was devastated. I clenched my fist. I wanted to kill this guy. He was over stepping every threshold of brutality.

"What's happening?" Jia asked me with a frown. She didn't have the ear-pods so was not aware of anything that scoundrel spoke

"He married that girl instead of Aroha on the same day. She is Aroha's best friend." I replied. Jia scrunched her nose in disgust.

"Don't show any mercy on him." She commanded. I nodded with deter-mination.

Tane had recovered from the push Aroha gave and marched towards them in anger.

"Kei te hiahia koe ki te whakatau i tetahi atu."

(You want to meet someone else.) Tane gritted, he again looked at that Drew fellow who understood what Tane wanted. He nodded and left. Again he dragged someone and dropped him near Tane. This fellow was badly beaten and was barely conscious. I dreaded and my fear turned true when Aroha screamed.

"Matua"

(Father) Aroha screamed and ran towards her father, shaking him to wake up

"E te poriro, i aha koe ki a ia?"

(You bastard, what have you done to him?) Aroha was crying badly. I can't take this anymore.

"Kaua e manukanuka kare ano ia i mate... ano. Ko te tangata rawakore ki te waha i to whiunga. Engari kaua e manukanuka i muri i taku whakamatenga i a ia, ko ahau te upoko o tenei iwi ko koe...ko koe hei rangatira moku."

(Don't worry he is not dead...yet. Poor man had to bear your punishment. But don't worry after I kill him, I will be the head of this tribe and you...you will be my mistress.) He chuckled.

He was about to lay his filthy hand on my mate but I yelled at him to stop. I just can't stand here and watch him do whatever he wants.

"STOP. Don't you dare touch her." I said walking toward them.

"Kare au i te marama ki o korero, engari ka whiua ano koe"

(I don't understand what you are saying, but You will be punished too.) He said confidently as if I will believe him.

"Leave the girls, be a man and talk to me. I know you understand what I am saying. So drop the act." I replied.

"You talk about being a man? You are just a kid and I will kill you with my bare hands" you humiliated me by snatching what was mine." he replied in English. His accent was a bit different but he spoke clearly

"Oh really? I would like you to try. I challenge you to fight me." I yelled at him.

He started laughing

"This is going to be fun. I would love to kill you." He smirked

"Let's see, who kills whom"

Hey everyone,

Thanks a lot to all who are reading this story and voting on it in spite of late updates

I am really grateful to everyone for your support and interest.

Hope you enjoy this chapter.

Thanks a lot.

The fight

Vincent 's pov

"Let me just finish him off, he talks too much." Aldrich said suddenly coming to life. Tane was blabbering to his people that When I die he should not be blamed and something on same lines

"Ohh your highness, Aldrich the great. Thank you for gracing us with your presence." I mocked him.

"Cut the crap human and let me fight him." He commanded

"No." I firmly replied to him.

"Excuse me. I am not asking you. I will fight him." He declared.

"Where were you till now, sleeping peacefully right? So go back to sleep. I will handle this. Thank you so much." I scoffed.

"Human, I..." he started to say something.

"Alpha's order Al. We will play this fair. We can't reveal ourselves to humans." I stopped him in the middle before he could complete his sentence.

"Who said anything about revealing ourselves to humans? Just give me control of your body. And you think he will play fair?" He replied

"I said I will handle him. He can't beat me." I put my foot down. Why the hell everyone thinks I can't fight Tane.

"As you wish. Don't come to me when..."

"I won't." I again didn't let him finish whatever he wanted to say. I know I can defeat Tane. He will die today.

"Hey you, whatever your name is get ready to fight " Tane called me with a smirk. He is so full of himself.

Everyone had moved out and formed a circle in between, Tane was standing in between proudly as if he was invincible. He can have all the glory till he gets smashed.

Bro patted my back. 'Go get him.' He mindlinked me.

Jia winked at me. 'Just get done with this fast. I want to go home,' she said in a bored tone.

I looked at Aroha. She was still holding Pania beside her father. She gave me a confident smile. I nodded, assuring her that I would win.

I stood in front of my challenger and stared at him.

"She shouldn't have brought you back. Look what that will result in. You, losing your life." He smirked and chuckled. I just stared at him.

"Don't worry. Cheaters are punished very gravely in our tribe." He stated.

"And what about traitors?" I asked looking deep in his eyes. His face twitched a bit and his nose flared, he was getting angry but he morphed his expression.

"I know traitors are not shown mercy anywhere in this world " I smirked this time. He furrowed his brows at me but regained his attitude again.

"You picked the best girl from our tribe. I must say you have a great taste. Just look at the girl that came with you, she is hot." I know he is trying to rile me to provoke and distract me by mentioning Jia in this.

"Ignore whatever he says" Jia mindlinked me. We were circling each other by now.

He stopped and took a stance by crouching, his one hand in the air stretched out and the other touching the ground. It looked like some kind of ninja pose. My eyes were focused on his every move. My ears were listening to every flex of his muscles . I could smell his fear, just a bit but it was there and that could be my advantage.

What he did next was never anticipated by me. He took some earth in his hand and threw it at my face. If not for my werewolf reflexes, I would be half defeated by now. I dodged most of it but still few particles got in my eyes, making me shut my eyes tightly. I heard a few gasps and yells.

"Are you okay?" came bro's concerned voice through mindlink.

"I am fine, bastard will pay for this." I fisted my hand.

"I told you he won't play fair." Aldrich commented. He was on full alert now.

"Ya, ya, I know." I rolled my eyes at him and tried to clean my eyes with my sleeves.

"Vinci be careful he is attacking you. On your right.". Bro cautioned me.

I heard the sound of his arm moving towards me from my right side and took hold of it before it could reach my face. I was trained for this. We trained a lot with blindfold to fight our opponents with just sounds that came from them.

Tane grunted and brought his other arm towards me and I took hold of that too. He was trying his best to free himself from my hold but was not successful. I kneeled him in his stomach and pushed his hands. I heard him stumble and land on his butt. Taking advantage of the time I cleared and opened my eyes. He was trying to stand up clutching his stomach.

I gave him time to get steady first and as he approached me again I kicked his knee. It made a satisfactory cracking sound. He screamed with pain and lost his balance, falling on the ground.

"You swine" he gritted and pulled my leg making me fall next to him. He pounced on me and pressed his elbow on my neck. He was fast and strong. I should give that credit to him. With one broken knee, he still managed to hold me down with his body weight.

———————

Hey everyone,

Thanks a lot for reading the story and liking it.

Next will be updated soon.

The fight part 2

V incent 's pov

"You swine" he gritted and pulled my leg making me fall next to him. He pounced on me and pressed his elbow on my neck. He was fast and strong. I should give that credit to him. With one broken knee, he still managed to hold me down with his body weight.

Our faces were so close, I could smell his breath. He pushed harder on my neck making my breathing difficult.

"Any last wish?" He smirked triumphantly.

"Y...yes." I banged my head on his forehead with full force. His grip on my legs loosened and I kicked his broken knee. He lost all his hold on me and I flipped us with me straddling him on his chest with both his hands under my legs. He struggled badly to free himself. I punched his jaw drawing blood from his nose. I punched him again.

"My last wish ...is to tell everyone your truth." I stated.

I punched him hard on his heart. He doubled and spluttered blood from his mouth. He was losing his consciousness. I stood up and made him stand on his knees, holding him by his hair. His whole weight was on his single leg.

"Tell your people what you have been doing. Tell them the truth." I gritted

He groaned and grunted, not opening his mouth.

"Waiho taku tama e te poaka"

(Leave my son you swine.) His father came rushing towards me but bro grabbed him.

"Tell them and I will spare your life. Tell them that you are selling young girls of your tribe for human trafficking." I told him

"N...nev" he tried to say but then started coughing badly.

"Me pehea koe e Tane? Me pehea koe e whakapohehe ai i to iwi ake? Kare rawa koe i whakaaro me pehea te tukinotanga me te whakaitinga. I tipu ake koe me ratou. Ko ratou to whanau... me pehea koe."

(How could you do it, Tane? How could you deceive your own people? You didn't even think about how these girls will be treated and humiliated. You grew up with them. They were your family...how could you.) Aroha came forward and spoke telling everyone his truth

"Me pehea... ka taea e au?... ka patai koe. I hiahia ahau ki te moni. I pirangi au kia mawehe atu i konei, mai i enei tangata katoa? Ka whakarihariha ratou ki ahau. Ko taku oranga i konei e whakarihariha ana ki ahau...I pirangi ahau ki te oranga ngakau nui me nga taonga me nga taonga papai. He aha kei roto i enei ngahere... he paru noa."

(How...could I?... you ask. I wanted money. I wanted to get away from here, from all of these people? They disgust me. My life here disgusts me...I wanted a lavish life with riches and luxury. What is in these forests... just dirt.) He spat and a huge gasp was heard from the crowd around us. They would have never dreamt that their future leader hated them so much.

"Tane... "his father was devastated hearing him talk about his life with such disgust.

"He pouri koe"

(You are pathetic.) Aroha gritted. She had tears in her eyes and it broke my heart

"Kati koe uwha... nau i pahua nga mea katoa. I te tuatahi i haere koe ki te whakaora i nga kotiro katoa, katahi koe ka oma mai i to maatau marena... ka kawea mai e koe to hoa aroha ki te whawhai ki ahau?... I whakaaro ahau ki te haere atu i tenei wahi ka noho ki te taone nui... taku...ka patua koe e ahau..."

(Shut up you bitch...you ruined everything. First you went and saved all the girls and I had to bear a huge loss then you ran away from our wedding making me look like a fool... and now you bring your lover to fight me?.... I had planned to go away from this place and live a luxurious life in the city...you destroyed my plan...I will kill you...) he hollered and tried to go towards Aroha but before he could go any further, I grabbed his neck from behind with my elbow, He started thrashing wildly to free himself.

"How dare you try to touch her" I increased my pressure on his neck. How dare he even think of saying those words about my mate. I will rip him apart before he could even lay a finger on her hair. While my whole concentration was on keeping the pressure on his neck, I never saw when Pania came and stood in front of us.

I furrowed thinking she would ask me to spare her husband. Plead to leave him and forgive him but then the way she was glaring at Tane said something else and before I could register what she was planning to do a hard punch landed on Tane's jaw.

There was pin drop silence everywhere. Even Tane was looking at her with shock. But he recovered and again thrashed to free himself gripping my hand

"E uwha, ka patua koe e ahau'(Bitch, I will kill you.) Tane barked

"Patua ia. Kare ona tika kia ora"(Kill him. He has no right to live.) She looked at me and whispered.

"ko ahau to tane"(I am your husband.) He screamed

"He pai ke kia pouaru ahau ka waiho hei wahine mau"(I better be a widow then be your wife.) She whimpered

————————

I thank everyone who is still reading this story, inspite of late and random update.

Thanks a lot.

True Queen

"Taronatia kia mate"

"taronatia kia mate"

"taronatia kia mate"

All the people around us were saying the same thing. I don't know what it was, I don't even know what Pania said because during our fight I lost my earpods and now I was unable to understand their language. It was frustrating to not understand at such a crucial time. My hold on Tane was still strong but he had given up on his struggle to free himself after he heard the crowd.

I glanced at everyone bringing my eyes back on Aroha with a question. She was still consoling Pania.

"Hang him to death. That's what they are saying." Bro explained taking in my confused glances here and there searching for answers.

"What did the girl say?" I furrowed at bro. Richard had left Tane's father and now he was slumped on the ground all defeated. I felt bad for him. No parent can see their child's death even if he deserves it.

"She asked you to kill him. She better be a widow then be married to him. Her words." he stated. Well what do you expect from someone who is forced to marry her friend's fiance and that guy turns out to be a traitor and to top it all he even destroyed your dignity in the name of husband's right.

I was confused, what was I supposed to do now, kill him as everyone was suggesting or spare him as I had promised Tane if he told everyone the truth. Which he did.

"Kill him Vinci, hang him to death because once a traitor is always a traitor." Jia said. I glanced at Aroha and she understood my turmoil. She came towards me and I asked bro to handle Tane, he also gave his ear pods to me. As I neared Aroha, she hugged me.

"I tino mataku ahau. I whakaaro ahau ka ngaro koe"

(I was so scared. I thought I would lose you.) She said against my neck. I pulled away and cupped her cheeks in my hands and touched our foreheads. I love her so much and it comes naturally to us werewolves but receiving the same intensity of care and concern from her in such a short time that we know each other, made me feel blessed. I could see in her eyes the level of love she holds for me in her heart. We may not have spent much time together but the feelings are eternal.Now I know why people go crazy for their mates. I chuckled and looked in her eyes.

"I told you nothing will happen to me. You need to trust me more." She nodded her head in response with tears rolling down her cheeks. This is the last time she is crying, I won't let her cry after this.

"Irihia ia, kei te hiahia to iwi ki te tika. Ko te hunga katoa i mamae mo ia e hiahia ana ki te whakawa."

(Hang him, your people need justice. All those who suffered because of him, need justice.) She said caressing my cheeks, I leaned into her touch, the warmth only she can provide.

"My people?" I furrowed wondering.

"Ae ko koe to matou upoko inaianei. I toa koe ki a ia, a ko koe to matou upoko hou"

(Yes you are our head now. You won against him and that makes you our new head.) She spoke with pride.

I was zapped for a second. I know I have to be a head, an Alpha one day but this was totally exceptional. I looked at everyone who was asking for justice through their eyes. They were betrayed, wronged. Their daughters were harassed and humiliated, their dignity was ripped away from them.We may not be able to wipe off the entire human trafficking racket but this has to be done to set an example for everyone who might think that it's easy to get away after any crime they commit. This will be a precedent of fear for those who should not even think of betraying anyone.

"Okay...let's do this." I told her with determination. She gave me a beautiful smile, nodding her head. She intertwined our hands and dragged me towards a small stone platform. She nudged me to stand on it. It seemed like a position for the head to address his people. I took a step on it and pulled her with me. She was reluctant but I forced her to stand beside me as my equal. She is more worthy of this place than me. She is the real queen, a warrior that goes to any extent for the betterment and happiness of her family.

She is my queen, my Luna and one day we will serve our pack in the same way. I was so proud of her.

"Today was a very difficult day for me. I had to fight for my love and for justice for everyone." I glanced at my love and kissed her hand

"He ra tino uaua tenei ra ki ahau. Me whawhai ahau mo taku aroha me te tika mo te katoa" Aroha translated to everyone with help of ear pods in a confident voice like a true Luna.

"And I am happy that I won. This was never a fight for being a head...no. It was a fight to prove myself worthy of Aroha and her love and if by winning, I became a head to you then I will take the responsibility... with honor. " I said and Aroha repeated it in her language a

"Having said that, we can never forget what Aroha has done for our tribe." I said and she looked at me.

"She is the most worthy person in every aspect to be a head of our tribe." I continued staring in her eyes. She was reluctant and didn't not translate what I had said.

"Say it." I whispered in her ears. She blushed and conveyed what I said.

"I want Aroha to take the rightful decision for the traitor. "

"Please Aroha announce your decision." I took a step behind her still holding her hand in mine and gave it a squeeze to show my support.

She sighed heavily and then held her head high.

"Ko ahau, ko Aroha Maunga, kua whakatau kia taronatia a Tane Maugham e whakapaetia ana mo ana hara katoa. Kia taronatia a mate noa."

(I, Aroha Maunga, have decided to hang the accused Tane Maugham for all the crimes he has done. To be hanged till death.)

Hope you enjoy reading this one.

Thanks for reading and voting and for comments.

Follow me to get updates

The Ritual.

"**Y**ou must be so happy, right"

"Yes"

"Feeling like a hero, on top of the world. Isn't it?"

"Yes"

"You won her heart and her people's heart."

"Yes" I was beaming with everything Aldrich was commenting on. He was praising me for a change.

"You became the head of their...oh sorry your tribe."

"Yes."

"What a great achievement isn't it?"

"Y..yes" I don't why but this is not going as I was thinking. Why do I smell sarcasm in his words?

"So I should give you a standing ovation. Right?"

"U...umm" this is too far-fetched. He will never give a standing ovation to me.

"And end this story here itself. Your happy ending. Forever...and they lived happily ever after. Isn't it?"

"No...no" there he goes to his real intention.

"Then you will have babies and...oops...you cannot have babies, I forgot. But you will have pups...PUPS. you hear that. You will have pups because you are a Werewolf. A WEREWOLF." He yelled at me as if I am not aware that I am a Werewolf.

"I hope you remember that and before you go all lovey dovey with our mate....OUR MATE. She needs to know about us, ABOUT ME. You get that. She is my mate too and I would like to at least let her know about my existence. I hope you are understanding..." Aldrich was apprehensive by now, shaking with frustration.

"Ya ...chill. I get that. I ...will..tell her....soon." I tried to cool him down.

"How soon?"

"S..Soon"

"Now."

"What?"

"Tell. Her. Now." He ordered.

"Are you crazy? She has already been through so much. You saw what happened here, still you ...I can't just go to her and say...come on. Be reasonable. We are in human settlement, I can't show her what we are. What if she panics and rejects us?"

"She can't," he resolved

"How are you so sure?" I asked him.

"Don't try to fool me here, she doesn't know how to reject and as a matter of fact she even doesn't know that she can reject so don't put any ideas in her head."

"Al. I will talk to her. Please give me some time. Please..."

"Okay"

"Okay?" What? He agreed? Just now he was getting impatient.

"Thanks"

He was really getting impatient. I know I need to tell her about us but so much was happening all of a sudden that I didn't get time to think on how to tell her without making her freak.

It was night time after finishing everything, that is punishment for Tane, They lit fire torches around to light up the area. Sky was clear with the moon visible and cool air was flowing. I looked around to search for Aroha. She was kneeling next to Pania and they were doing some rituals. It was like praying to their goddess, yes they too worship a goddess named Hinekapea she is goddess of loyalty so they pray to this goddess to forgive the sins of the person they give death punishment to. So after Tane was ...um hanged, each and every member of the tribe prayed in front of his dead body for forgiveness of his sins and to give his soul peace and place in heaven. They also ask forgiveness for themselves as they punished the person. I think it's very thoughtful. Aroha said that the soul should not be punished for what the body committed. It's very deep but also touching.She asked me to join but I declined stating I don't know their prayer which they were singing together. The scene in front of me was surreal. The whole ritual was surreal yet serene. The song they were singing in chorus and the fire that was lit in center as it was night time, the sight that displayed faith was giving me goosebumps. It was mesmerizing.

"I can't believe, I am witnessing something like this...it's so....so...I don't know what to say...but it's giving me goosebumps." Jia said, rubbing her arms. She was leaning on Richard as We were standing a bit far leaning on the trees and watching their ritual.

"I can feel it too, the goosebumps." I replied taking deep breath

Richard huffed and looked at me. There were a thousand questions in his eyes and it felt like he was thinking which one to ask first.

"What now?" He asked the most difficult one. How do I answer it? I myself am not sure. What now? It feels like a sword hanging on my head, like a stone stuck in my throat.

What now?

"I don't know...maybe I will ask Aroha to come with us...or"

"First, she needs to know about us." He commanded. It irritated me and made me angry.

"Do you think I don't want to do that? I want to, okay but it scares the shit out of me. I don't know how she will react...what if...what if she rejects me?" I yelled letting go of my frustrations.

"Vinci...I know it's difficult and you are scared but the more you delay it, the more it will complicate your relationship with her." Jia tried to make me understand and it's not like I didn't realize it but still... I looked at the moon goddess for strength. Even after winning against Tane I feel defeated.

"And then you have to go to Alpha training camp for two years also, so better make it fast." Alpha announced.

____

Hey everyone,

A very Happy New year to all of you and may this year is full of happiness and opportunities for you.

My new year resolution is to give regular, timeline updates and finish this story. I hope I achieve it.

I know, I am loosing readers because of my rare updates and I am so sorry for that. This year it's going to change.

I will give regular updates and you all please vote and Follow me.

Thanks

Training camp

V incent 's pov

"And then you have to go to Alpha training camp for two years also, so better make it fast." Alpha Richard announced.

What the actual fcuk? I had forgotten all about the training camp in all this chaos. That camp will be for two years. Two fcuking, freaking years. 730 Days! How will I be able to go away from my mate for such a long period. It's not possible I won't go. I can't I can't stay away from her for such a long time. And the most freaking part is that you cannot leave that camp in those 2 years. No meeting family, no going out...nothing. Hah! Not going to happen. We hardly know each other and there are so many matters to be discussed. This is so annoying. I still have to tell her about who I am. I don't know how she will react and how long it will take me to convince her... and in middle of all these how can he expect me to go away...that too for two years

"I won't go." I stated as if it was so simple and moved into the forest

"Excuse me! What did you say?" he growled, coming behind me.

"I won't go to that stupid camp, leaving my mate for 2 years. It's just not possible." I stated with irritation still continuing to walk

"It's not an option. You have to go to become an Alpha..."he fumed but I didn't let him finish.

"I don't want to be an Alpha then." I yelled getting agitated

"Have you lost your mind? Do you even know what you are saying " he came and took hold of my arm making me face him.

"You won't understand how it feels to be away from your mate for so long...you didn't have a mate when you went to that camp. So don't..."

"Are you defying your Alpha? Don't you forget I am still your Alpha and you are bound to me." He hollered in his Alpha voice. I had to summit to him

"Y..yes Alpha" I replied bowing to him.

"Better. You will go to Alpha camp for 2 years and get trained there to be the best Alpha. Got it?" He commanded in a calm Voice

"Yes, Alpha."

"Hmm." he hummed and went away straightening his clothes. I and Jia looked at eachother.

"Vinci..." she tried to say something but I stopped her.

"Don't...just don't. You always take his side and never say anything for me. So now don't go on telling me that he is right. He was never in my situation." I snapped at her.

"You don't know. Okay so don't judge people on half truths." she fumed.

"What do you mean?" I asked.

"I...I am not his first mate." she choked looking at the ground

"WHAT? What ...I...never knew that he had a first mate? What happened to her?" I blurted. How is it possible?..like...he never said anything. This is difficult to believe.

"Not my story to tell, you better ask him." she went away saying that. This is so much to take. I was not able to control myself and Al was getting agitated. so I ran from there, deep in the jungle and shifted, running faster. I just ran and ran fighting against the wind. I need to clear my mind.

We need to clear things out. I told Al.

He ran even faster, his paws hitting the wet mud of the forest rigorously. He was furious that we were going away, that we will be away from our mate. I need to calm myself before I confess to Aroha.

I mindlinked Jia that I will come directly to pack house and they should not wait for me at the tribe. After spending some time in solitude near our territory I went home. As I neared the house, I shifted back and wore the shorts kept near some trees. I saw bro sitting on the steps of the pack house and smoking. He rarely smoked that too away from his kids and mate. I went and sat beside him, he passed his cigarette towards me. I hesitated a bit as I had never smoked before.

"Take it, it helps." He instructed.

I kept it between my lips and inhaled as I had seen him do. As soon as the smoke filled my lungs, it suffocated me, making me cough badly. He patted my back as if it was the most mundane thing to do. My cough subsided after a few seconds and I passed his cigarette back to him.

"I will manage without it." I scoffed and he just shrugged it away. The air was getting colder and carried the moist smell of the forest. I inhaled deeply, gaining courage to ask him.

"Wh...who was she?"

"Someone from our pack. I never met her." He shrugged.

"You remember the rogue attacked us when I was at the Alpha camp?" he asked me

"Yeah"

"She died in that attack. I felt a heart wrecking pain and Derek told me that we lost our mate. It was painful. I was depressed for a month."

"You never told anyone"

"Ahh, things our stupid young self do." He chuckled. I didn't get what he meant by that.

"I wanted to be an Alpha and I thought if I told dad, he won't give me the position because there is no Alpha without his Luna." He elaborated.

"Oh! Seriously?" I furrowed.

He chuckled again and got up.

"Go and sleep, it's getting late." He ruffled my hair and went inside.

"Jia served you right." I huffed. She was not ready to accept him as her mate initially. Alpha Richard had to kneel and beg for his love.

"She was asking for you." He informed me and he went away. I just nodded knowing he was not there to see it. I just left from there without meeting her. What must he have thought? I took a deep breath.

'Aroha. We need to tell her everything.' Aldrich sighed.

I will tell her everything, and will even go on my knees and beg for her love if needed.

Hey everyone.

We are almost at the end of the story. Hardly 2 more chapters are left.

If possible do vote, comment and follow.

Missing her.

Two years later

Vincent 's pov

Two years, two fcuking freaking years, 720 days, has passed and don't expect me to say that they passed away in a Jiffy, because they didn't. I have died every second of it as it passed. You can never imagine what it feels to be away from your mate for 2 years. I wanted to burn that camp down so many times. Even, I had tried to escape from there, these dogs guard it so well. There were two more future Alphas, Kadan and Lucas. They too had just met their mates and had to come here leaving them alone. We have become thick friends, rebels in the eyes of authorities. Hah we made their life hell. We used to trouble them so much thinking they would kick us out but it never happened. And here we are after finishing our training all set to head home and meet our mates.

Aroha...I have been literally breathing her in me. Not a moment passed when she was not in my mind. Finally I will meet her. I want to kiss her and love her, mate her just take in her fragrance and fill myself with it. I will hug her so tight and won't leave for days, no months...yes

"Hey buddy you leaving?" Kaden asked, coming with his luggage.

"Yes, finally." I replied loading my luggage in the trunk of my care

"Hope to see you again Vincent" Lucas patted my back

"Ya of course, you both will receive an official invitation to my ceremony." I bro hugged them

"Sure buddy." They said going towards their vehicles.

I remember the day two years back so clearly.

Flashback.

I went to Aroha 's tribe the next day and asked around for her. People there guide me to a newly built house. It was very beautifully decorated. I wondered who it belonged to. Debating whether to go in or wait in front of the doorway I saw Aroha coming outside. She saw me and squinted her eyes in anger. I knew I would face her anger as I went away yesterday without meeting or even informing her. She started walking inside and I followed her. I need to be calm today.

"Aroha" I called her twice but she pretended to not listen and went inside a room where she started arranging clothes in the niche formed on the wall for storage. Is this her house? I glanced around but it was a totally empty room. Is she shifting in this house?

"Is this your house?" I asked

"Inaianei kua tae mai ia ka hiahia ki te korero" she mumbled with her hand literally throwing clothes inside. I didn't understand anything.

(Now he comes and wants to talk)

"Umm...are you shifting here?" I tried again. Does she want us to stay here and live here?

She furrowed her brow and looked at me.

"Y..your...ho..house?" I asked gesturing my index finger around the room

"Taku whare? He aha tenei hei whare moku huh? Ka noho ahau ki te wahi e noho ai koe. Ka noho ahau ki te waahi kei to kainga. Porangi" she mumbled

(My house? Why will this be my house huh? I will live where you live. I will live where your home is. Idiot)

"No my house", she said in English. Before she again starts rumbling in her language I fumbled the earpods out of my pockets and gave it to her. Damn, I need to learn her language. She snatched them from my hand and placed them inside her ears. I too wore another set

"I hea koe inanahi? Me pehea e taea ai e koe te haere pera i muri i nga mea i tupu. Kua ngaro noa koe....I" she started as soon as the earpods reached my ears.

(Where were you yesterday? How can you go away like that after what happened. You just vanished....I)

"Aroha, I need to tell you something." I said loudly. It made her stop talking and look at me. Her dark eyes held fear and confusion. I went towards her and cupped her face. Her eyes teared up. Why was she so scared?

"Can we go outside and talk" she nodded just then Pania came inside the room and saw us. She bowed her head saying sorry and went away.

"Ko te whare tenei o Tane. Nana i hanga mo matou engari i te mea ko Pania tana pouaru, ka noho ia ki konei. Ko ta matou tikanga ko te tane tane e hanga whare mo tana wahine a muri ake nei"

(This is Tane 's house. He built it for us but as Pania is his widow, she will stay here. It's our custom that a groom builds a house for his future wife.) She explained.

"I will build a house for you too." I whispered near her ears.That spread a beautiful smile on her face and it turned into a cute blush on her cheeks. What was there to blush in a statement of building a new house?

I looked at her with confusion and she blushed harder not meeting my eyes."Ka taea e te tane marena te whakaoti i tana marena i muri i te tuku whare ki tana wahine marena hou. He tohu mo to raua hononga" he mumbled.

(A groom can consummate his marriage only after gifting a house to his bride. It's a symbol of their connection.)

"Oh"'Bloody Bastard! He built this house thinking about touching our mate.' Al yelled in my head. That enraged me too. I want to kill him all over again.

"I hiahia koe ki te korero i tetahi mea?"

(You wanted to say something?)

"Ya let's go." I took her inside the forest.

I made her stand a few feet away from me and faced her. She was so confused.

"Okay... please don't run away...please don't be afraid. I will never harm you...and please don't hate me... "I told her. I was so scared. I don't know how she will react and what will happen afterwards!

"Please don't run away." Saying that one last time,I started removing my clothes. She was shocked and held her head low.

"Vincent e kore e taea e maua i mua i te marena" She hid her face behind her hands.

(Vincent we can't before marriage.)

Before I could tell her that it was not what she thought, Al had taken over and I was shifting already. Now I was just a spectator because what Aroha spoke will be totally irrelevant to me and she can never know what Al was doing.

Al grunted to get her attention. She looked at us with wide eyes and took a step back. Oh no,. She was gonna run away. But then her wide eyes didn't hold any fear or dread. They were in awe, absolute awe with what she saw. I know she is fearless but then too anyone will be afraid if they saw a man turning into a wolf, a big ass wolf.

'Not our girl' Al smirked

"Aue taku atua"(Oh my goddess)

"He pono tenei? He pono nga korero katoa. Kaore au e whakapono. Aue!"(Is this real? All the stories are real. I can't believe it. Wow!)

"He wuruhi koe Vincent?'(You are a Werewolf Vincent?)

I just heard my name and a smile crept up on her lips. Oh goddess this girl is something. Her eyes were dancing with amusement.

She knelt in front of me and extended her hand, a bit reluctant to touch. Al moved forward and kept his head below her hand. Her touch was magical; it brought a tingling sensation on my skin.

Al grunted again, making her flinch.

'Don't scare her.' I yelled at him.

'Do you think she is scared even a bit?' Al sassed back. That was so true, her eyes were mesmerized.

"Aue taku atua….Aue taku atua"Oh my goddess….OH MY GODDESS. Aroha squealed as I shifted back to my human form

She bowed and touched her head on the ground in front of me

"Hey, what are you doing?" I inquired. She is my Luna, my mate, my equal. Why is she bowing?

"He wuruhi koe! He mea hanga motuhake na te atua o te marama. Ko koe te manaakitanga. Kei te tuohu noa ahau ki mua i tona atuatanga."(You are a Werewolf! A special creation of the moon goddess. You are the blessed one. I am just bowing in front of her divinity.)

I hugged her but after few seconds she started wriggling

"V.. Vincent…koe…e tahanga ana koe" she stuttered.(V.. Vincent…you…you are naked.)

I chuckled remembering how she had left me there and ran away.

I went back to the house where Pania was staying. After knowing who had built the house and with what intentions, I didn't like it a bit and the decor too was okay, nothing great. We talked and then I informed her about the camp. She was so heart broken and cried a lot. I wanted to kiss her so badly but refrained myself because I would have not been able to stay away from her after tasting her lips.

Oh goddess I should have gone to her tribe instead of coming to the pack house. My whole body was aching for her touch. My eyes have gone sore after not seeing her for two years.my heart feels lifeless without her embrace.

I parked my car and came out. Jia was the first one to greet me. She took me in a warm embrace. Goddess I missed home. Bro came and hugged me next. Can you believe it I missed him too.

My little mumkins were the next to pounce on me. I hugged them so tight, inhaling their smell. I swear never to go away from them. Everyone came and hugged me..Dal, Hunter, Wayne, mom dad all. I miss everyone so much.

"What are the preparations for?" I asked as saw lots of workers arranging things and moving around

"Off course for your welcome party." Mom beamed

"Welcome party...but..." I reasoned, I want to go to my mate.

"No but and no if. Go and get fresh." Jia commanded. Now how can I deny my Luna. I huffed and went to my room. Oh I missed my room too but it smelled a bit different

"Welcome back Vinci. I hope you are never leaving again for so long." I turned around when I heard that voice and got the shock of my life.

Hey everyone, hope you all are doing well.

So this is the last chapter of this story. Next will be Epilogue.

It took forever to complete this story, I don't know why. I hope you enjoyed reading this one inspite of delayed updates. I truly appreciate you all for keeping you interest in the story.

Please vote and do comment to let me know your feedback

Thanks a lot.

Epilogue

<hr>

V incent's POV

"Welcome back Vinci. I hope you are never leaving again for so long." I turned around when I heard that voice and got the shock of my life.

It was Aroha, standing right there in front of me. My heart skipped a beat. She was looking breathtaking in skinny jeans and white crop top. I just didn't know what to do or say or....I was stunned. I was looking at her after two whole years. I had recreated this scene in my head so many times but when we are actually in front of each other, I am so lost. My breathing gets heavy with each passing second. I am scared of my reaction. I don't know what I would do if I touched her. I don't want to come across as a desperate teenager but the pull is so strong. The whole situation is so overwhelming... we both are just looking at each other's eyes, her's are brimming with tears.

She takes a step forward and I take one step ahead. I don't know how long we were just trying to reach each other but when she placed her palm on my chest, I lost all control.

I engulfed her in my arms breathing in her scent as if it was my oxygen. I can't survive without her. Oh goddess how did I even stay away from her for two years. I tighten my arms around her, hiding my face in her hair.

"Vincent" she choked.

"I tino mihi ahau ki a koe." I said in her language.(I missed you so much)

She pulled her face away and looked at me with amazement.

"What, only you can learn my language? I learned yours too." I told her. Yes, I learned it during my stay at the camp. I had two whole years to master it. We can't just depend on a device to communicate for our whole life now, can we?

"Good for us, now we don't have to use that device" she chuckled. I cupped her face and touched our heads. Her warm breath fanned my lips. My eyes moved to her wet trembling lips. They were so inviting and before any rational thought could stop me I placed my lips on hers and there were fireworks exploding inside me. This was my first kiss ever which I had reserved for my mate and I am so grateful that I waited for this moment because it was totally worth it. We just stood still, not moving our lips a bit then she moved away a bit and looked in my eyes. Those brown eyes were filled with love and desire. She whimpered when I hungrily attached her lips with full force again. She took a step back due to the impact but I placed my hand behind her head and the other hand around her waist making her body flush against mine. She was shocked initially but then put her fingers in my hair. I sucked and nibbled her lips as if my life depended on it. The kiss was full of urgency and longing. We had been apart for so long it reflected in that kiss. It was sloppy and messy, our tongues got tangled and teeths were clanking but nothing was stopping us.

After what felt like forever, we moved apart breathing in the much needed oxygen. Aroha was breathing heavily, her chest moving up and down. I was losing my senses. The urge to mark her was building in me, my canines were itching to get extended. I pulled her closer and sucked the skin of her neck where my mark will be there. She moaned a bit and I grazed my canines on her skin but the very next second she pushed me.

"Vincent, you cannot mark me now. It has to be done during the Alpha ceremony." she almost yelled.

"Thank goddess, Jia would have killed me..." she continued moving away from me.

"What?...Alpha ceremony?"...How does she know about our ceremony and rituals?

"Yes. The ceremony of our titles is next week. You have to mark me there and I won't be able to mark you but still there will be an oath ceremony for me..."

I was so confused...how does she know all these things?...

"How do you know? Wait a minute, how long have you been staying here?"

"For more than a year now."

"You have been staying here? In my room? In this pack house for more than a year? I mean...how...why...?"

"Jia came a few months after you left and said that I need to get trained as well for my Luna title as you are being trained for your Alpha title. So I came here with her and since then she has been training me about werewolves" she shrugged.

I took a long breath. This is so...overwhelming. She has been staying at pack house, learning all about us and getting trained to be a Luna. I just kept staring at her. I love her so much.

"I love you." I hugged her saying that. She giggled and replied, "me too" in my ears.

"Let's go downstairs. Everyone must be waiting" she dragged me with her.

———

Two days later we were driving...somewhere. No one told me where we were heading. Bro was driving with Jia beside him. Me and Aroha were in the back seat. Even she was aware of the destination. Cool, let's get surprised then.

We reached the construction site of a huge beautiful house. It was almost completed, just final coloring was going on. I somehow had slept through the drive and was totally unaware of where we had reached.

"Where are we?" I asked getting out of the car. All three of them went inside without replying. I followed them like a lost puppy.Goddess what are they up to.

As I reached inside. Hunter came and hugged me. Then Dal too came and hugged me.

"Welcome Alpha to your new pack house" bro came and hugged me.

"What?" I was zapped.

"Yes, our new home. Pack house of Northern moon pack." Dal informed me with pride.

"Oh my goddess. Seriously? You all made the pack house too. Is there anything left for me to do? I...I don't know what to say."

"You liked it?" Jia asked

"Ya it's amazing" I told her honestly. It was a beautiful house full of amenities and modern interiors. It was truly spectacular.

"Aroha helped a lot with the design and details." Jia informed me and all of them went inside the kitchen space. I held Aroha's wrist and pulled her towards me. She wrapped her arms around my neck and kissed my cheeks.

"You liked it?" She whispered

"Wasn't I supposed to build a house for you?" I asked tucking her hair strand behind her ears.

"Yaa, but you know times have changed. Women are getting better at things than men." She sassed

"Is it now? Are women getting better at kissing too?" I asked leaning to claim her lips

"After the ceremony" she pushed me.

Ahh this ceremony I groaned

Finally the day of ceremony arrived. It was held at our new pack house which was completed just yesterday. All the members of the Northern moon pack shifted here yesterday itself. All of the Southern Moon pack was present. Whole event was so tiring. All of us took the oath, then we were given the title of Alpha and Luna, we marked each other, (Aroha gave me a bite too. It just left teeth marks on my neck) Beta, Gamma and others took their oaths too. We went for the run as well.

By the time everything was done it was already past 2am. Aroha went to change her dress in our room. It was a beautiful white gown, she looked like a moon goddess today. And now no one has any right to stop me from doing what I have been craving for years. Tonight is the night.

"I am so tired, I am not even able to keep my eyes open." Aroha said coming out of the washroom in a silk nighty. Damn she is so beautiful. I inhaled her fragrance and it was endgame for me. She went inside the comforter and slept within seconds.

Excuse me! This is not how it was supposed to be right? I panicked. How can she sleep? I went and sat beside her on the bed and tried to wake her up twice but she was in deep slumber. I huffed and stood up. I was so frustrated that I wanted to yell and throw things around but somehow I managed to calm myself. Maybe she is really tired.

"Better luck next time human" Al snickered.

'Just get lost.' I yelled at him in my mind and threw myself on the bed. After a few minutes Aroha turned towards me and kept her one hand and one leg on me. My whole body was burning with the close proximity and She was sleeping peacefully smuggling to me. I moved her away and tried to get up but then she held my wrist, stopping me.

"I thought it's our wedding night and you are leaving me alone?" She pouted and made a cute face.

"You slept first and now…"I yelled in frustration and she started laughing at me. Oh so all this antics were to pull my leg is it. I will show her now. I pounced on her and that made her stop laughing.

"I don't see you laughing now?" I kissed my mark on her neck and she moaned.

And we mated of course. I just can't wait to live my life with her. With my Enigmatic mate who was such a big mystery for me when we met. From being totally irrelevant to each other 's language and customs, today we know everything about each other. We will face ups and downs in life like every mates and like every Alpha and Luna but we will try our best to come out as winners

Hey everyone this is the end of their story. Hope you enjoyed reading.Al pha Vincent and Luna Aroha lived their life happily ever after.

I will be posting bonus chapter but it may take time.

Thanks a lot for reading this book